MMXIV

THE WHITE REVIEW

| | |
|---|---|
| EDITORS | BENJAMIN EASTHAM & JACQUES TESTARD |
| DESIGN, ART DIRECTION | RAY O'MEARA |
| POETRY EDITOR | J. S. TENNANT |
| ASSISTANT EDITOR | BELLA MARRIN |
| ONLINE EDITOR | TYLER CURTIS |
| EDITORIAL ASSISTANTS | HANNAH PHILLIPS, OLIVER TAYLOR |
| | |
| CONTRIBUTING EDITORS | JACOB BROMBERG, LAUREN ELKIN, EMMELINE FRANCIS, |
| | DANIEL MEDIN, SAM SOLNICK, KISHANI WIDYARATNA |
| | |
| FUNDING & DEVELOPMENT | SOPHIE GORDON |
| | |
| HONORARY TRUSTEES | MICHAEL AMHERST, DEREK ARMSTRONG, HUGUES DE DIVONNE, |
| | SIMON FAN, NIALL HOBHOUSE, CATARINA LEIGH-PEMBERTON, |
| | MICHAEL LEUE, TOM MORRISON-BELL, AMY POLLNER, |
| | CÉCILE DE ROCHEQUAIRIE, EMMANUEL ROMAN, HUBERT TESTARD, |
| | MICHEL TESTARD, GORDON VENEKLASEN, |
| | DANIELA & RON WILLSON, CAROLINE YOUNGER |

COVER ART BY CHRISTIAN NEWBY
PRINTED BY PUSH, LONDON
PAPER BY ANTALIS MCNAUGHTON (OLIN CREAM ROUGH 100GSM, OLIN WHITE SMOOTH 120GSM)
BESPOKE PAPER MARBLE BY PAYHEMBURY MARBLE PAPERS
TYPESET IN JOYOUS (BLANCHE)

PUBLISHED BY THE WHITE REVIEW, APRIL 2014
EDITION OF 1,500
ISBN No. 978-0-9927562-1-5

THE WHITE REVIEW, 243 KNIGHTSBRIDGE, LONDON SW7 1DN
WWW.THEWHITEREVIEW.ORG

# EDITORIAL

THIS TENTH EDITORIAL WILL BE OUR LAST. Back in February 2011, on launching the magazine, we grandiosely stated that we were 'creating a space for a new generation to express themselves unconstrained by form, subject, or genre'. In laying out these aims in a preliminary editorial, we in fact constrained ourselves to the tedium of having to come up with something interesting to say with each new issue, having set the precedent.

In our second issue, we announced that 'we are not yet in a position to pay contributors, (or ourselves for that matter)'. Thanks to an Arts Council grant awarded earlier this year, the former is no longer true: we are now able to pay writers and artists a small fee for their work, both online and in print. As for paying ourselves, our naïve dreams of wealth and fame soon proved illusory – and there's always the spiritual reward to be reaped in solving 'technical, mechanical issues ... in a small room, surrounded by paper' (*THE WHITE REVIEW NO. 3*), with the art director Ray.

Our fourth editorial was probably our most rousing ('We hope that you find something in this issue to provoke or inspire you to pick up a pen, a paintbrush, or a placard'), and most embarrassing ('The future is there to be forged'!) considering that you are likely to land on a picture of Juergen Teller's scrotum on opening the issue. While that photograph may have been an attempt to combat the notion that 'literary and arts reviews are in London considered decidedly unsexy' (*THE WHITE REVIEW NO. 5*), no 'wild parties ensu[ed] thereof', despite the editors' best efforts.

By December 2012 our editorials had run out of steam, which perhaps explains why our call for trustees to join our charitable board was ignored. Despite stating that 'any reaction is a gratifying one', we received none. Aggressively pursuing new board members is clearly not our forte, but we like to think that 'forcefully demonstrating the vitality of literary culture in Britain and Ireland' is. At the time of writing, the editorial staff are working through several piles of submissions to the second White Review Short Story Prize, the tottering heights of which are testament to a thriving writing culture on these isles.

In the eighth issue, published last summer, we boldly declared that 'all evidence of any manifesto ever drawn up by the ... editors has, happily, been destroyed'. This was a brazen lie: the evidence remains, safely stored on one of the editors' hard drives, and goes a long way to explaining the mystery of the camp heron imprint that perches on the inside cover of each edition of the magazine.

By last November, we were so uninspired by editorials that we proclaimed that issue's 'boring' in the third line. Faced with the same blank page a few months later, we despaired. So it is here, in our tenth issue, three years since we launched, having published hundreds of stories, essays, poems, interviews and series of artworks, in print and online, after having spent too many late nights in a small room with Ray eating cheap pizza and arguing about semicolons, after having worked tirelessly to topple the establishment to let a new talented generation *unconstrainedly* express themselves, that we must take our leave from you.

There is an African proverb that goes, 'Everything has an end, apart from the banana, which has two.' The editorials have come to an end (until we decide otherwise); THE WHITE REVIEW continues. From now on, if you want to hear from us, come to the events.

THE EDITORS

# GERONIMO

BY

## BENEDICT ANDREWS

*Nowhere.*

– We're on the ground.
– What?
– Landed. We've –
– We what?
– The boys've landed. They're in the compound.
– On the ground.
– Ok. Gotcha.
– Right on.
– What?
– He said, right on.
– Oh yeah right. Right on.
– Is he?
– Shh. Nothing, it's nothing.
– Right on right on.
– Are you sure he's – because I'm –
– It's fine. He's fine.
– Right on baby.
– He's just –
– What?
– Excited.
– Are you sure this is –
– It's fine – what we – it's fine.
– Watch. Just shut up and watch.

*Pause.*

– Looks good.
– Looking good.
– Yep, look-ing gooood.
– It's pretty –
– Yeah pretty much what we.
– Good picture.
– Yeah nice.
– What we –
– I like the colours.
– Yeah nice. The colours.
– Real pretty.

– Sublime.

*Pause.*

– Ok – watch – ok – ready?
– Ow.
– Ouch.
– Ouch. That hurt.
– That hurt alright. High five.
– Do you want – does anyone need?
– Nah. I'm fine.
– All good.

*Pause.*

– Right on.
– Right on.
– Yeah, right on.

*Pause.*

– Don't wanna –
– What?
– Don't wanna, and this is crucial –
– For sure.
– Don't wanna mistake her hysterics for genuine –
– No fucking –
– Emotion.
– Way.
– Hell no.
– Claw.
– What?
– Claw.
– Claw?
– Yeah, like she's clawing.
– On her back – trying to claw –
– The what? The –
– Air. Clawing the air.
– The air. Face.

– Does she think it's a face? Think someone is – what? – on top? On top of her?

– Think she can claw – can claw her way –

– Claw the face off.

– Claw her way the fuck out of there?

– Out of thin air.

– Threat. She's a –

– Weapon, she's got –

– Thin air.

– Ouch.

– Not moving.

– Not so busy moving now.

– Not so busy with *movement* now is she.

– Clawing.

– Flailing.

– Like – like a –

– Not so busy now.

– No.

– Christ.

– Jesus fucking Christ it's down.

– Oh fuck, fuck, fuck.

– Oh fuck, oh Christ.

– We lost one.

– It tilts, hovers and –

– Oh Christ, it can't –

– Fuck fuck fuck.

– Down.

– Hangs. Suspended. Like a –

– Bang.

– Down.

– The blades touch the –

– Concrete.

– And it's over.

– Over and over.

– Torch it.

– Over.

     *Pause.*

– Fine. We'll be fine.

– Us? Of course we'll –

*Pause.*

The boys? Yeah right the boys. Of course they'll be fine. The boys.

*Pause.*

– Hey guys.
– What?
– People are worried.
– What?
– Worried, they're worried.
– Worried? About what?
– The name.
– What have people got to worry about?
– The name.
– We're doing this to make them safe – safe fucking safe – not worried. For Christ's –
– Worried we got the name wrong.
– It means some things to some people and might give the wrong you know.
– The name?
– The name yeah. The mission name.
– Fucking people. Which fucking people?
– Well.
– Which fucking people think we got the name wrong?
– Sensitivities. Cultural –
– Overfuckingsensitivefucking.
– Which people which fucking people?
– Indians. The Indians.
– Native.
– Native – sorry – Americans.

*Pause.*

– To them it means something, some kind of hero. Not a villain.
– Definitely not a villain, monster, target.
– Ok. Ok.
– Resistance fighter. Hero.
– Ok.

F

*Pause.*

– Sorry?

– Say sorry?

– Sorry say sorry? Who to? What have we got to be sorry about?

– Lawful. Legitimate. Appropriate in every way.

– Ok.

*Pause.*

– Yes. Right. Ok.

– Nice.

– Nice one, did you see that? Nice one.

– All clear.

*Pause.*

– I'm like you. Pretty much normal. A normal guy. Like everyone else I worry my life is going nowhere. You know. Not where it should. The wrong direction. Lost. When I was a kid I thought I'd grow up to do all these you know *amazing* things. Like everyone else. I worry about my weight. What I eat. Chemicals. And the melting. I flew over Greenland once. This chunk of white. Jesus. I felt so small. Strapped in my seat. Helpless. Wow. I like to swim and after I've done my laps I go into the steambath. Relax. Just sit there and sweat. Light was coming through the glass bricks. Man wow. These slats. Shafts. Golden like heaven. Wow. And one of the guys was sitting there, legs crossed, real still. He didn't move for like ages. Fucking forever. Like he was *praying* or something. Finally. Finally he leaned over. Bent over so I saw his back. And on his back tattooed was Jesus Christ in all his suffering. Nailed. The thorns. And I thought, holy fuck, this is like – like *what is this*? Some kinda *training video*? Because I want to believe. I long to believe and the steam, the golden light, the Suffering Christ. Was this like some kind of *message*? A SIGN? I thought ok I get it. I get this. I could really get into this. I mean I want to believe as much as anyone. The light. His wounds. I'm so lonely. Lonely all the – even with my friends – my *wife*. I'd do anything to belong. To feel that. You know – bond, belief. Like them. In their deserts. Praying in their huts. And air–conditioned compounds. For a better life. To be given, sent, a *sign*. Some sign that it's all worthwhile. Hasn't been for nothing. The suffering. Because otherwise what? Oh my fucking. And then what? The body now without spirit. Meat. No longer one of us. Please please not that.

F

*Silence.*

– Worn out, exhausted, dead tired, finished, at the end, wasting away.
– Yes.
– But elated.
– What?
– Worn out, exhausted, dead tired, finished but elated.
– At the end, wasting away.
– But elated.
– Yes.

*Pause.*

– Live.
– What?
– It said, it wants to live.
– What said what?
– It – he – said, live. Please let me live. I want to live.
– Fucking.
– Let me live. Let me live. Please.

*Pause.*

– Don't do this. Please don't.
– No way.
– No way buddy.
– No way he's becoming a goddam *martyr*.
– Saint.
– Not fucking well one of the *prophets*.
– No way. Not going down like that.
– Don't say –
– Going down – don't say –
– Ok ok. Not parading him. No way.
– Show him? What? Like a show trial?
– No way.
– Trial ha.
– Martyr.
– He's not the victim here.
– Inspire.

F

– Please. No one needs to actually see him –

– Ha.

– Alive or dead.

– We got him.

– We got the guy.

– Got him we got him.

– Hell yeah.

*Silence.*

– She came home drunk. I'd been waiting for hours. Fallen asleep somehow. Well not really asleep. I mean how can I sleep when I don't know where she is. Not asleep no. Anyway when I woke up from dozing or whatever, she was just *standing there*. Slurring words. 'Sorry? I've got no reason to say I'm sorry.' She said. 'I don't have to say sorry ok.' Could hardly even talk properly. I must've dozed off again because when I woke the bed was empty. Well, I dragged myself out of bed to go see if she was alright and there she was in her party dress asleep. Upright. Sleeping upright in her party dress. All crumpled dress. Drooling. On the couch. Drool on her party dress. Passed out like that. Laptop open on her lap. Screen asleep. I wanted to know what she'd been looking at. Drunk on the couch looking at what while I slept in the other room? In our bed. What? What was so important? I wanted to know but I didn't wake up the screen and look. I didn't do that. No. I shook her. Shook her and shook her. She just wouldn't wake up. Rag doll in her pretty party dress. Wake up. Saying her name over and over. Shaking her. And when her eyes opened, she looked at me but said nothing. Like I was really far away. Like at the other end of some corridor. A shadow at the other end of some corridor with its blinking light. Pixels. I got her on her feet. Lifted her up. And she she she wandered off in like completely the opposite direction. Away from our room. I don't know where she thought she was going. No idea. I've never seen her like that before. Not like that. So blank. Anyway the next day she sat on the couch, make up all smeared. Her lips looked like she'd been kissing. Who? And on tv, they replayed the raid. Dust. She was in shock. Some kind of *shock*. Like she didn't know what had happened. How she got like this. We talked about our way of life. How we wanted to live. She said she needed to feel free. She didn't want to feel like she had to justify herself all the time. It's her life she can do what she wants. We just had to you know like *believe* it would work out. And it would. She didn't want other people telling her how she should live. I.e. what was possible. Or not. No. She didn't want to be *held down*. This scene I saw recently. Someone. Was it a film or live footage? A clip of a real event? Anyway this actor, this guy – it was out of focus, grainy, blown out – and he, this guy was holding this other guy down and he –

F

*He demonstrates.*

Was repeatedly striking the guy on the ground. Lifting this brick up and down and destroying the other guy's head. Up and down again. This happened. I think it was real. This white brick in his hand.

*Silence.*

I wondered how long she would just sit there talking about personal freedom.

*Silence.*

Eventually she crossed the room and knelt at my feet and rested her head on my lap as if this was the only way to make me understand that she was sorry. Because words had failed her now. She needed me to understand that she didn't want to lose me. I held her head in my hands like a glass ball that at any moment I might lift and drop. I held her head and stroked her hair. I told her that she was precious to me. Very precious.

*Silence.*

– And the body falls.
– Tumbles.
– Weighed and shrouded.
– Into the receiving sea.
– Like?
– Like an old package.
– An aid package.
– Food.
– Sorry?
– Food.
– Like food.

*Lights fade.*

# INTERVIEW

WITH

# CAMILLE HENROT

CAMILLE HENROT'S WORK IS HEADY AND HUMAN, mixing and merging cultural codes in a variety of media like an incarnation of Laplace's demon, seeing interlocking connections that stretch from one end of the universe to another. Her deep and abiding interest in anthropology provides a useful handle for understanding the artist's meta-critical approach to systems (cultural by default), the resulting hybridity of her work, and her concern with how humans are and can be with the world, themselves, and one another. A paradigmatic example of these themes in her work can be found in her utopic *EST-IL POSSIBLE D'ÊTRE RÉVOLUTIONNAIRE ET D'AIMER LES FLEURS?* [Is it possible to be a revolutionary and to still love flowers?], a series of often extraordinary ikebana accompanied by citations from books in her personal library, a selection of which were reproduced in *THE WHITE REVIEW NO. 5*.

Beginning her career at the prestigious École nationale supérieure des Arts Décoratifs, where she specialised in video animation, the young Parisian artist continued to focus almost exclusively on video work until some six years ago. In 2010, she was nominated for the coveted Prix Marcel Duchamp, for which she exhibited 'Coupé/Décalé', a film that has literally been cut in two, leaving one side of the image, in which Vanuatu natives jump into the void with nothing but liana vines tied to their feet to secure them, perpetually out of sync; a 'navigation chart' based on a traditional Melanesian object and made of brass water heater pipes; and a minimal collage featuring the tarot card 'The Hanged Man' affixed to a magazine spread of nude women engaged in sports, harkening back to the jumpers of 'Coupé/Décalé'.

I met Camille Henrot the following year when she was looking for a translator. Our exchanges following this led to a friendship and some balked attempts at collaborating on a text connected to her *TROPICS OF LOVE* series, consisting of drawings of male, female, human, animal, and vegetal hybrids with very prominent genitals. After working together on a layout featuring her ikebana series for *THE WHITE REVIEW*, Camille told me about a project on 'the history of the universe' which she would be undertaking thanks to a fellowship from the Smithsonian Institute in Washington, DC. She spent countless hours researching at the Smithsonian, reading creation myths from around the world, and looking through potentially useful images – to the point that the stream of images continued even when she closed her eyes. We collaborated on a sort of poem that would become the voice-over to the video that resulted from this fellowship, 'Grosse Fatigue', which was awarded the Silver Lion at the 2013 Venice Biennale.

Despite the imminent opening of her latest exhibition, *THE PALE FOX*, at the Chisenhale Gallery and her plans to take over the second floor of the New Museum in New York this summer, Camille was able to make some time to meet with me in a room of her mother's apartment that she transformed into a makeshift studio during her last trip to Paris.

Q. THE WHITE REVIEW — What kinds of feelings do you want an artwork to give you?

A. CAMILLE HENROT — I like it when I don't understand. I remember Gabriel Orozco's exhibition at the Musée d'Art Moderne de la Ville de Paris, and I remember the style of it was connected to the idea of stimulating the brain. I like it when an artwork stimulates my brain. When I say the brain, I don't just mean the cerebral and the conceptual. Art has to be like that.

Sometimes you see something and you are deeply uncomfortable with it. The first time I saw Ryan Trecartin's films, I couldn't understand because of the way the people speak. There is something very aggressive and vulgar and complex about it. I remember that at first I didn't like it, and then I realised that I did like it but I was not able to formulate why. I think Proust wrote about that in IN SEARCH OF LOST TIME, about the idea that beauty is very often what you cannot put into words. The narrator is invited to see la Berma, the singer he has been dreaming of hearing, but when he goes to see her, he is not overcome by pleasure. At first, he is disappointed by the experience, and then he realises that he's not disappointed but over–stimulated by her singing. He doesn't find a category into which to put his experience, so he first judges it as a bad experience before later coming to realise that this is the true experience of art. I like it when I feel that, but it means I'm never able to make my judgement very quickly. I'm always careful about that. It happens very often that it's only with five years distance that you realise that a work was really impressive and influential – but you didn't see it at the time.

Q. THE WHITE REVIEW — What have you made that you would never sell?

A. CAMILLE HENROT — A lot of things. A lot of drawings. Many ikebana – the ikebana exhibition was not a very commercial gesture, and it was not meant to be.

Q. THE WHITE REVIEW — What about your sculpture 'Le Balafré', which you made after seeing and subsequently coveting a second–century Persian sculpture at the Louvre? I imagine it is rather personal.

A. CAMILLE HENROT — No, it's a bronze edition, so I can have one and other people can still have one, too! I really like working on patinas with bronzes, and the guy who makes bronzes with me is a patina specialist, so we always work on the edition in a very interesting way. The patina doesn't vary a lot between different editions, but it does vary, and I like this idea. I'm doing a series of new bronzes for my show at the Chisenhale Gallery, called DESKTOP SCULPTURES. They are inspired by objects you would find on your desk – objects that are used as paperweights or tape dispensers or bookends, or that represent power or trophies, or even plants.

Q. THE WHITE REVIEW — Are the objects abstract or are they rather familiar?

A. CAMILLE HENROT — The separation between what is abstract and what is figurative has never made a lot of sense to me. I never really do abstract things, because even if it's an abstract form, it's related to a feeling, and so it's not abstract. I don't believe abstraction exists. I consider that as human beings, we are not able to think abstractly. Even if you think about numbers – one, two, three, four, five – and the way they are taught to children, there are colours connected to them. Like, four is red. And you can even attribute genders to them, four can be feminine. In the book THE PALE FOX by Marcel Griaule and Germaine Dieterlen, for example, which is an anthropological book on Dogon cosmogony that was one of the very big inspirations for the voice-over in 'Grosse Fatigue', four is the number that represents the female principle, while three is the number that represents the male principle.

Q. THE WHITE REVIEW — What do you think of the number seven?

A. CAMILLE HENROT — I would say it's the number that represents totality. In a lot of cultures, seven is the number that represents totality and fourteen is a number that represents 'many'. I think all humans have this knowledge of seven representing everything: there are seven days in a week, and the number seven appears in many important texts across civilisations. It's completely embedded in any time you pronounce the word or you see the number visually – it is immediately connected.

Q. THE WHITE REVIEW — Your work often feels as if it is bursting at the seams with information. Other than learning that there is lead in the water supply, or something like that, does the face value of any one piece of information ever effect a change on how you live, or does your very keen awareness of the codes that form and are formed by information mean that you maintain a critical distance?

A. CAMILLE HENROT — I feel as if being aware of the codes is a mode of survival, but it doesn't make anyone happy. The more information you have access to, the more unhappy you're likely to be. 'Grosse Fatigue' – even just the title – is connected to this. In mythology, too, knowledge is something that makes people unhappy. I wouldn't say this is always true – in Rabelais, for instance, it's the opposite. Literature and poetry give me so much pleasure because they are forms of knowledge that are fulfilling. Anthropology or philosophy, by contrast, are

always stimulating and a little therapeutic, but at the same time they add to your problems. Knowledge is a kind of drug that makes you unhappy but also gives you a sense of relief. I feel like that's my general relationship to information – I get excited about an idea temporarily, I'm happy about discovering new things, and then it slowly becomes too much. I am also frustrated to perceive the limits of my own access to knowledge. Any experience of building knowledge is always frustrating. It's very banal and I hate to say it, but the more you know, the more you discover you don't know. Perhaps it's like in the book of Lieh-Tzu, where you learn everything and then at one point you decide to stop speaking and you start being happy and forget everything.

Q. THE WHITE REVIEW — Can you tell me more about the show you have at the Chisenhale?

A. CAMILLE HENROT — The show is called THE PALE FOX, and it's a continuation of the research I did at the Smithsonian. It's a show that's about global projects and the desire to totalise everything into a single object or, in this case, into a single exhibition.

Q. THE WHITE REVIEW — How does it depart from 'Grosse Fatigue'?

A. CAMILLE HENROT — The Chisenhale show is an exhibition with only objects. It developed from a frieze of aluminium sheets that are displayed in a rhythmic way. The exhibition is set to ambient music. It's meant to be an experiment in fighting the limits. That's why I was interested in ambient music, because you feel like everything is merging. The title is THE PALE FOX, as I was interested in this concept of the pale fox as the element of disorder in order – the necessity of integrating disorder into order and how this is somehow the principle of creativity. It is about building a system, but accepting that the system is arbitrary and will be threatened by disorder. This is the experience of making art.

Q. THE WHITE REVIEW —— And where do you go from there?

A. CAMILLE HENROT —— Many directions. I didn't want to do a safe show where you have a very nice sculpture and background and a conceptual field all around. I wanted the exhibition to be a sort of grid, where the cardinal points are attributed to Leibniz's principles and to the different ages in a human's life: childhood, adolescence, adulthood, old age. With this very schematic approach to the space, I'm displaying 190 objects I bought on eBay on the aluminium shelves I designed, which are less shelves than a kind of musical score. The whole exhibition is very related to the idea of total art, so it's an experiment for me. I was interested in working to the very end of the idea of combination.

Q. THE WHITE REVIEW —— Do you feel you're coming to the end of combinatory practices? The mixing and merging of disciplines, media, and cultural codes has very often been said to be a core element of your work.

A. CAMILLE HENROT —— I would love to, because I feel it's a nightmare. Sometimes I dream of just doing painting – just very minimal, gestural painting.

Q. THE WHITE REVIEW —— Would that not be satisfying now?

A. CAMILLE HENROT —— I feel it would be very satisfying, but maybe I will wait until I am wiser. Right now there are still so many images, objects, shapes and sounds to deal with that I want to embrace the possibility of dealing with many elements. I put together an exhibition in very much the same way that children play, distributing objects in a circle and attributing them functions in a narration. I decide, 'Okay, so I'm going to use this image and it will be connected to the idea of the beginning and after that there will be this transformation that happens.' It reconnects to the idea of narration in space, as with a frieze in a cathedral.

Q. THE WHITE REVIEW —— I like the non-proscriptive aspect of your work, which allows for any number of meanings and connections to bubble up.

A. CAMILLE HENROT —— A work of art can be received and interpreted from a variety of angles. That's why I have always been interested in codes. A code, with its system and its opacity, allows for many interpretations. I always try to make work that can be read in many different ways, which is why it's often very useful for me to write in anticipation of making anything. I go through all the different directions in my notes and it's only through writing about it that I come to understand which directions I feel are more interesting to push and which ones less so. My problem is stopping – it's always difficult for me to renounce any possibility. When I say it's a problem, I really mean it, both in terms of organising a show and in terms of my sanity. It's exhausting to go in all directions because it takes more time, and more work, and more money. I came to understand that it's interesting to push it far and then see what happens, but I'm not sure I can continue doing that for very long. Maybe it's just a momentary thing and I will shift to a very focused, simple and wiser practice. You're told to focus on one thing or to do one project, but actually there is the option to do a lot – of course you can't do everything, but you can try. When I was doing research at the Smithsonian,

I discovered it was an option not to choose, and this attempt to achieve the impossible is what makes art interesting. This question of limits and of attaining the impossible through the exhaustion of all possibilities is something I am working through now, but I know that it is not going to be possible to continue this forever.

<sup>Q.</sup> THE WHITE REVIEW — Is it just a question of not having time to think it all out from every angle, of not being able to always run through the manifold associative meanings evoked by a given concept, be it 'hair' or 'East' or 'childhood'?

<sup>A.</sup> CAMILLE HENROT — Yes. I discovered that the grid, this very ordered system, is a way to maintain all possibilities. Because the grid represents the total aspect of life and universe, it's a way for me as an artist to reconnect with the arbitrariness of the gesture. The exhibition addresses that: the relation between order and disorder, the arbitrary and the sensible. These are questions that you can't escape right now, just as a consequence of being in contact with the internet and its constant streams of images. It's like gymnastics – your brain needs to build connections, because if it didn't it would be scary. But the more you build connections, the more arbitrary things become. This making of sense can only end in the acceptance that the arbitrary is a law of the continuity of things. Order is still there, but it doesn't have to be in order all the time – it exists, but it doesn't have to be followed.

<sup>Q.</sup> THE WHITE REVIEW — So it's more of a local organising concept that can itself change?

<sup>A.</sup> CAMILLE HENROT — Yes. I've always been interested in feng shui and how Far Eastern thinking fascinates the West – how Far Eastern practices are sometimes perceived as a remedy to the problems of Western civilisation. I made a series of engravings called THE GOLDEN LEGEND, for example, with Christian martyrs in yoga positions. And then when I worked on the film 'The Strife of Love in a Dream', it was also a work on the reciprocal fascination between East and West and the therapeutic effects of this relationship.

<sup>Q.</sup> THE WHITE REVIEW — What artists have influenced you?

<sup>A.</sup> CAMILLE HENROT — I've been influenced not only as an artist, but as a person by Yona Friedman and Pierre Huyghe. And Martial Raysse.

<sup>Q.</sup> THE WHITE REVIEW — You worked as an assistant to Pierre Huyghe, didn't you?

<sup>A.</sup> CAMILLE HENROT — Yes, but for a very short time. At that time, I didn't think I wanted to be an artist. Even after working for him, what I wanted was to make music videos and films. Later on, when the films I made were better received in the contemporary art world, I started thinking about my experiences working for him and I realised that the way he was working, his hesitation and his consideration of all the different possibilities, was very close to my own way of doing things, and that's how I came to think that maybe I should continue working in contemporary art.

<sup>Q.</sup> THE WHITE REVIEW — How did you make the move from video work to objects?

<sup>A.</sup> CAMILLE HENROT — When I met Yona Friedman and was spending a lot of time at his home trying to prepare a film, I started looking at all the objects he was making out of other objects. When I was at art school, people would say I drew like I was Japanese, because it was always very graphic – very flat, like the negation of the idea of 3D. And then,

when I looked at Yona Friedman's models, I noticed that he also had this very pictographic way of drawing, and he was doing 3D models out of this very flattened position of things. I felt comforted by the idea that you could do 3D objects with a really flat graphic approach to volume, and so that's how I got interested in making objects.

Q. THE WHITE REVIEW —— Was it around that time that you got into working serially as well?
A. CAMILLE HENROT —— It's very hard for me to produce only one work. When I'm invited to participate in a collective exhibition or a biennial and I have to produce just one work, it's extremely painful because of my incapacity to turn away from a possibility. I like to build environments with many objects.

Another reason I build these environments with many objects is because of the way we live in apartments: there is a lamp, and a table, and a seat, and something on the desk, and a curtain, and so on. I'm interested in the domestic aspect of space. The museum space is so empty and disconnected from life, and I'm interested in making art that reconnects to a feeling of being home. The ikebana project was very much about that. It's a protected environment, but it's also protected from reality, which a home is not.

Q. THE WHITE REVIEW —— Do you usually start a project with a kind of magnetic seed that pulls other bits towards it, or does everything coalesce all at once?
A. CAMILLE HENROT —— Very often, I try to protect my first intuition from all other preoccupations. And very often in my way of working, I find elements that reinforce this intuition and so I try to be as open as possible for this to happen. That's why I really like the habit of collecting on eBay, because these

things seem to come to me, because I just happen to find this or that. I like this idea of objects coming into my life and thinking about why they would arrive when they do. In a way, I try to read into objects like some people practice divination, trying to read the way water spreads out and collects on the floor, or how a cat moves, or the stars. Even when I make films, it's related to this.

Q. THE WHITE REVIEW —— Why do you think you've taken to reading objects from eBay instead of reading the stars?
A. CAMILLE HENROT —— Well, we're living in a materialist world, and so the world of objects, the world of supply and demand, and of auctions, really represents our environment.

Q. THE WHITE REVIEW —— Do you 'Buy It Now' or do you buy through auction?
A. CAMILLE HENROT —— I buy through auctions, but sometimes I 'Buy It Now'. It's more fun with the auctions, of course. It's interesting to see which objects have the 'Buy It Now' option and which are auction items. It's very often the things that have no value or too much value that are 'Buy It Now' – objects that are considered to have permanent value or lack of value – whereas the objects that are sold in an auction style are sold that way because the seller thinks that subjectivity might raise the price.

Q. THE WHITE REVIEW —— Your collage 'The Hanged Man' features the eponymous tarot card. Do you have a particular affinity for The Hanged Man?
A. CAMILLE HENROT —— When I was nominated for the Prix Marcel Duchamp, it was something that I perceived as a very violent experience. There are only two possibilities when you are nominated for a prize: you can

lose or you can win, and I've never liked binaries. It's difficult for me to accept that there would only be two possibilities. At that time, I was interested in the symbols of the tarot and in The Hanged Man's representation of failure. In a way, failure can also be perceived as success, because failure is the ability to renounce and to surpass your own desire, and this is a victory. I thought it was interesting to connect the figure of The Hanged Man to some yoga positions when you're on your head and you know what it means to see things from another angle.

Q. THE WHITE REVIEW —— How did you go from the tarot, which is a symbolic system with a pool of pre-designated meanings, to your exhibition at the Chisenhale with Leibniz and the incorporation of many different symbolic systems at once?

A. CAMILLE HENROT —— I'm fascinated by the failure of systems, and it feels like the minute you put one system next to another they both become wrong. I found it interesting to try to combine different systems into something that works, but it can never work. The work you and I did on the text for 'Grosse Fatigue' was very much about how sometimes it was impossible to build a consistent narrative out of so many contradictory narratives. In the end, the perception of it is that there is absolutely no authority because we are surrounded by so many possibilities. I like Leibniz because he was obsessed by this question, by how different possibilities can coexist in a single system. I feel like, as an artist – and I'm not a philosopher – I'm trying to see if this can work, how you can build an aesthetic where all the different aesthetics are combined together and will this collapse completely or can it hold together? This is why I say that the Chisenhale is a total experiment. It's not meant to be a successful exhibition, it's just meant to be an interesting experiment.

Q. THE WHITE REVIEW —— Do you find yourself trying to break apart your own systems, your own habits, or do you rather build on them?

A. CAMILLE HENROT —— I've never tried to fight any of my habits, but I probably should. I always try to be as free as possible with my work, but there always comes a moment when I want everything to be in order. But then I discover that it's going to be boring if it's too orderly, so I let disorder come back in again. So there's this back-and-forth between a freestyle, intuitive practice and a more grounded and elaborated style. It's always a changing and moving thing.

JACOB BROMBERG, FEBRUARY 2014

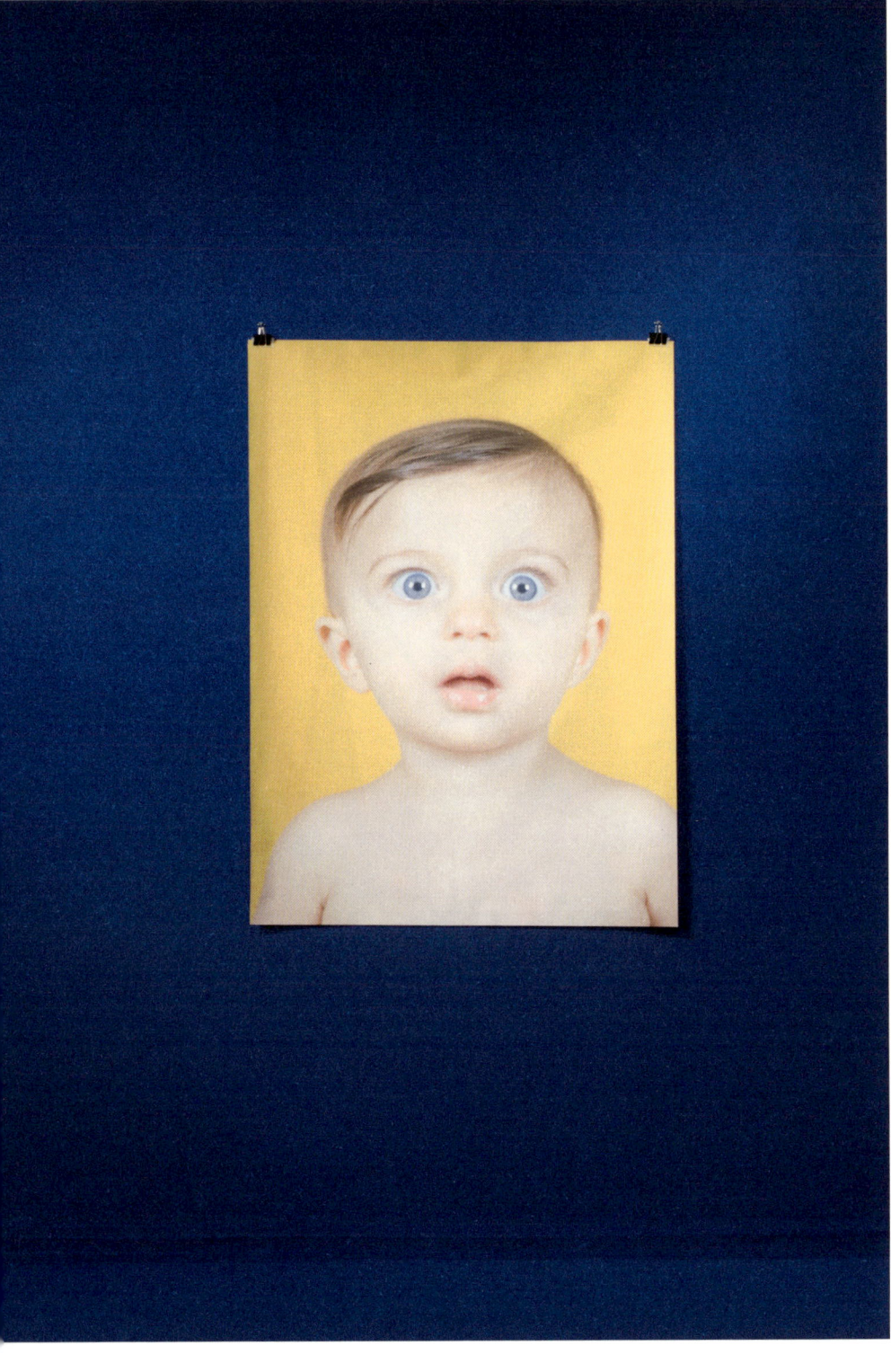

# POEMS

BY

## WESLEY ROTHMAN

## VIDYAN RAVINTHIRAN

## MARK PRINCE

## LAURA ELLIOTT

## BUTTERFLY SONG

*Dalí to Lorca*

Our deep songs ring rumble across Catalunya, Federico.
      The green hills and coastlines shoulder our music

like broad-framed elders, the whipping hems of flamenco
      down south. How we rowed through the Gulf of Roses

under Mediterranean heat and mist. How we rose from water,
      paddling air for a brown star setting.

We knew the sun, Federico, its private rendezvous
      and slow melting time. We collected steaming

drops from the clock of light, don't you remember?
      You burnt the shore with that light, split

deserts and coliseums open, vaporised every leaf.
      Every branch became a crutch, tined and waiting

for some body to lean, Federico. The rules transmogrified:
      pomegranates cracked out fish

that consumed tigers. Butterflies spun out the wind.
      Bodies turned to temples – which was always

True – to marble columns
      the air might pass and whistle through.

I wandered through your temple, Federico, after it was busted
      by rifle butts, riddled by the tyranny of gunfire,

its awful shrieking. The body was lost to the wind,
          carried into golden time on the backs of green hills.

And when I walked down from the mount, sat bent
          for the seaside, I saw you sailing off,

capturing the breeze in all your enormous butterfly sails.

## SELF-PORTRAIT AS GOLD GRIOT

*in the voice of Basquiat and the memory of Langston*

I lay me down as blood of the wood – sap essence. My people
strung every stitch of this cloth, every woven twist
of my shoulders. We've spun fibres from bark, dug roots
in the dark of short summer nights. Ellipses on every finger

cradle rivers five miles deep. I paint me down with bones,
flesh giving way. With bones, dab the colour and drag
the curves of ribcage and pelvis, skull–sphere and column–
spine. All the ceremony on my face – circles and wave–lengths –

tells our ringlet history. I saw the trunk from its stump –
every ring hides hundreds more, every lip splits for the blood
of my name. Every eye collects stories told on shoulders,
by elbows, in the shake of knees and neck turns.

Reenactments of reenactments reenact themselves, spun
into the circles of our children's eyes – spheres, irises, pupils
swum through by the rich black fabric.

## THE SKY

there was a uniform
inactive grey,
except when stared at
through a chainlink fence;

those who could
kept dogs
to be led around by,
affecting blindness

and pitied the students
of ancient languages
their wealth
of particles. No one thought

outshone the mica;
once the chancellors
learned to tweet
the incident

turned to harmless fun,
the spice of banter
hustled into sachets
stored in one's top pocket just in case.

## ART

As I approach the man in the painting
starts to cry
over what happened
with the little crickly
crackly sound
a dead fly
makes when you pick it up.

Poor bloke,
tied to instances
with a bluish–white blob
for an elbow...
It's about time
he put the kettle on
or had a thought
about a woman's lips.

The fly
begins to fizz
in the trash.

                    ‒

If you could paint
the sunlight on the wall
your whole life long
and never grow
a business, or bored;
breathe some clouds onto the blue...
But here comes
the middle of things.

                    ‒

We've been waiting for some time
– but for what if not more of the same?
Trying to appear
predatory and also faintly bored,
like the wallpaper at Wilde's remark;
some discover art for art's sake
after not before
they lose it all. Some are the trashed fly
and others, the middle of things. . .
most are brought aboard
by work and love
before they grasp what they already have.
Don't you cry before it happens.

## SZCZECIN

We were trammed or bussed through the old city.
The bridge carved, balustraded, lined with posters
of miraculous designs, solving many of our perennial problems.
I would have liked to alight and take a closer look
but bearded young men were marching towards the confluence
with a purpose it seemed inadvisable to interrupt.
Their milling suggested a foregone opportunity,
an unlived life – mine, not theirs – proceeding unregarded,
and too far gone to be reembarked on, with better results,
at an earlier point in its development. Never the sound
of a radio, a siren, a car door slamming,
only the chirp of women's heels, asserting their wishful prosperity.
The park sighed, exacting a response. Snaps, crackles, blusters
folding into more substantial echoes. It was a get-out clause
leftover from a more lenient and impoverished era.
Your wish to be pleased by what you happened to discover
was your special vulnerability. Goggle-eyed birds,
alert to every movement, remained motionless themselves.
At dusk, we came upon a district which left your eyes prospecting.
Now I see it persisting as though you had stayed.

## VARANASI GHATS

and who knew our skin could be so
   soft so early rinsed
in the sun's indiscernible *not* rising with the bells again
   always the bells and the dogs
  biting each other's faces
and the river drinking dawn as it mixes mist and milk as *chai*
   in clay cups on the stone steps –
  and this isn't what I meant
or noticed it was the chill in the city of fire, your gentle sleeves
   and the acid in my stomach
  threatening, latched onto
the night before – it could have tasted like anything like nothing
   *would you like to try?* folding
  cumin seeds coriander leaves
into dough for chapattis, half a watermelon's meat dripped
   on a new white dress we knew wouldn't
  stay clear for long –
as the light feels more like a leftover staining the new hours new skin
   smooth as the transition
  we barely noticed between
sharp garlic stars infusing the cushioned sky the rising bread
   dawn's uncompromised summon of palms –
  and what else was important?
that we went back to bed, my stomach a stew I poured
   hot milk into and threw the inhabited
  cups away after only one use

# THIS STRANGER STILL MOVING CLOSER

I read *chartreuse* and it is a bolt into the afternoon –
orange peel unfastened and the sudden scent in the air –
do you understand?

Blue eyes brown skin honeyed mind I wonder
and the white sky wheeling
around the wind–turbines like cotton

ungraspable as the desert in the desert.
It slips away in phases so that I can't believe
in distance

but think there must be a petrol station somewhere
selling sweets and cigarettes, I'm almost sure.
Sound flattens against sand.

Where is Chartreuse?
It is not the desert
It is not even the desert.

At intervals we all pause, unpack our saddles,
the fabric wrappings piled on the ground
as the camels ankle–bound fox–trot into scrubland.

We lay the saddles down like shells,
a brief installation, as the wind
re–sculpts the impermanent horizon.

Afternoons we misunderstand one another –
boredom in the desert! –
the body stirs in the temple.

Chartreuse is a big grey cat with yellow eyes,
it is the pink flowers with white buds
whose milk can blind you

– besides, I am in love.
Beneath the prickled heat and thorny branches
we each try to enter the landscape.

The desert is a hangar for flightless things
but the camel shells are beautiful
and have a meaning, unfolded –

stilted sacks of tea and turmeric potatoes.
In photographs they slump
convincingly, almost breathe.

Chartreuse is the clumps of nettles
that look like thin white spiders,
our fondness for the shade of this tree.

After we told the long joke about the tractor
and lay down in the damp blankets,
he started screaming *chartreuse!* in the moonlit dunes.

We led him back with our voices
(the camel man and me)
while you pretended to sleep (did you see the stars at 4am?).

The shepherds chew red beetles,
the goats chew on nothing discernible.
I mean chartreuse only.

# VERN BLOSUM, PHANTOM

BY

# WILLIAM E. JONES

CHATSWORTH, ESTABLISHED IN 1888 in the northwest corner of the San Fernando Valley, took its name from the family seat of the Duke of Devonshire. The developers who subdivided this part of Ex–Mission San Fernando, formerly called Rancho El Escorpión, preferred to associate themselves with England's landed gentry rather than with the poisonous arachnids native to the place. As in Hollywood, another formerly rural tract absorbed into the city of Los Angeles, efforts to elevate the tone of the area were never entirely successful. Companies producing mainstream entertainment, including the one responsible for the television programme *24*, have maintained offices in Chatsworth, but they have generally been overshadowed by the more enduring presence of the sex industry; besides many porn studios, the trade publication *ADULT VIDEO NEWS* has its headquarters in the neighbourhood, and sex toys are manufactured there. Most recently, Chatsworth distinguished itself as the place where the figure of Vern Blosum, a painter whose work achieved notoriety in the early 1960s, started to emerge from obscurity.

In February 2006, Jon and Tina Cassar bought a painting that looked like Pop Art, as anyone would say: a realistic depiction of a parking meter captioned with the text 'Twenty Five Minutes' (the amount of time left on the meter) in the kind of plain block letters used by professional sign painters. Jon Cassar, a producer of *24*, which consists of hour–long episodes unfolding in an hour of real time, must have felt almost as though the painting, with its image of a finite period time about to expire, had been made expressly for him. The Cassars' notes describe the circumstances: 'Purchased, Twenty Five Minutes, Vern Blosum 1962, at a price of $10.00. In Chatsworth, CA. At a corner storage lot. Due to storage container being vacated. Unknown reasons why. Unknown owner. Maybe due to no longer paying rental storage fees or could be it was left unclaimed.' After taking the painting home, the new owners found on the back of it a label reading, 'L. A. Co. Museum of Art, LOAN CAT 88, MR. & MRS. L. ASHER.' In the course of their first internet search, they found another parking meter painting, 'Time Expired' (1962), which had been exhibited at the Museum of Modern Art, New York. Thus began their research into 'Twenty Five Minutes' and the artist who painted it.

Further inquiries yielded references to three exhibitions in which Vern Blosum had participated. *THE POPULAR IMAGE*, organised by Alice Denney, at the Washington Gallery of Modern Art, 18 April – 2 June, 1963, included a series of paintings of parking meters at fifty, forty, thirty, twenty, and ten minutes before expiration, with a final painting entitled 'Violation'. *POP ART USA*, organised by John Coplans, at the Oakland Art Museum, 7–29 September, 1963, included 'Twenty Five Minutes', 'lent by the L. M. Asher family, Los Angeles'. *MIXED MEDIA AND POP ART* at the Albright–Knox Art Gallery, Buffalo, 19 November – 15 December, 1963, included a parking meter painting called 'Mass Violation', lent by the Sonja Henie–Niels Onstad

Collection. After these three shows in one year, there are no further references in Vern Blosum's exhibition record, with a single prominent exception.

¶ By far the most substantial traces of Vern Blosum's artistic activities are at the Museum of Modern Art Department of Painting and Sculpture, which retains a file on him. The earliest item in the file is a letter from dealer's assistant to client's assistant dating from the period when 'Time Expired' was acquired by MoMA:

Leo Castelli
16 February, 1963

Dearest Eileen,
The address of Vern Blosum is
1088 Center Drive
South Elgin, Illinois

He is 27 years old - no one has seen him.

Love,
Constance Trimble

E

This statement did not satisfy the curiosity of Museum of Modern Art director Alfred H. Barr, Jr., who was puzzled that Vern Blosum did not attend the opening of MoMA's new expansion on 25 May, 1964, and who furthermore suspected some sort of trick was being played on the museum. As he was preparing a new acquisitions show that would include 'Time Expired', he sent the following letter to Castelli in late September 1964:

```
                              Mr Alfred H. Barr, Jr.
                              Museum of Modern Art
                              11 West 53 Street
                              New York City




Dear Leo,
We are toiling on our collection catalogue and want, of
course, to be as accurate as possible. Several innuendos
and indeed some flat statements have led us to think that
there is something phony about the identity of Vern Blosum.
Would you please write me a letter signed by you giving
some biographical data on the painter of 'Time Expired':
full name (no pseudonym), sex, date and place of birth,
art training, present address and any other information
you may think relative. Hoax or no hoax, I like the
painting which is now on view - but our catalogue
is a serious record.

Yours seriously,
Alfred H. Barr, Jr.
```

E

Castelli managed to get Blosum to respond to this adamant request; he wrote back to
Barr three weeks later:

```
Leo Castelli
4 East 77 St • New York 21
14 October, 1964
```

```
Dear Alfred,
Enclosed herewith is a terse auto-biographical note
that we just received from the elusive Vern Blosum.
I hope it will prove to your satisfaction that he
is not a phantom.

Kindest regards,
Leo Castelli
```

The following is the text of the autobiography Castelli enclosed:

Born in Denver, 29 April, 1936
Parents died at early age, moved from relative to relative
First real job was running cars into Mexico for resale
Later became a used car salesman.
No formal art training, learned all I know from a friend,
who taught me the fundamentals and encouraged me to paint.
After five years of intensive work, I moved to South Elgin
to be near my friend.
My hobbies are flying and reading. I had a plane but lost
it when I decided to devote my full time to painting and
couldn't make the payments.

Two days later came a response:

16 October, 1964

Dear Leo,
Though the autobiography of Vern Blosum would certainly
not hold up in court of law as evidence of his existence
I suppose this is the best we can do to account for the
legend that our picture was painted on a bet by a student
at Pratt. As you know, we wrote Blosum, addressed the
letter to South Elgin, Illinois and received no reply.
In any case, I appreciate your efforts.

Sincerely,
Alfred H. Barr, Jr.

E

The terse autobiography sufficed to assure Barr and others at the museum; Vern Blosum's painting went on display, and it remained on view at least until the late 1960s. A *NEW YORK TIMES* article by Milton Esterow, 'Lunchtime Art Lovers Flock to the Modern', dated 31 August, 1967, mentioned 'Time Expired' and included a comment from Blosum: 'It's a series of time paintings culminating in a giant expiration.' The article does not specify whether Blosum's words came by letter or telephone or in person, but however the message reached the newspaper of record, it aroused no suspicions there.

And yet, the staff of the museum continued to have their doubts. Finally in 1973, a full ten years after the spate of exhibitions featuring Vern Blosum's works, MoMA sent a request for a birth certificate to the State of Colorado Department of Health, which responded with a form letter stating, 'We have searched our records but do not find a certificate of birth for: name, Vern Blosum; place of birth, Denver; date of birth, 29 April, 1936.' Thus the file on Vern Blosum at the Museum of Modern Art comes to an end.

Independently of the Cassars, and nearly four years after their initial inquiries, Greg Allen posted the question, 'Anyone Tell Me About Vern Blosum?' on his modern art blog, greg.org. He posted several instalments in his continuing investigation of Vern Blosum from January 2010 to September 2011.

Allen, who explored the archives thoroughly, discovered that 'Time Expired' had been purchased by the Museum of Modern Art with a gift from Larry Aldrich,

> whose foundation fund was set up precisely so that MoMA's curators could acquire works by unknowns like Blosum... Aldrich had set up the funds to get museum curators "to sort of do my shopping for me," he said. It was his impression that MoMA "had people combing New York galleries all the time", but that was "not the case".

Allen continues, 'In 1962–3, Pop was the new hotness, and MoMA bought because Castelli was selling. He was the one who had people – notably director Ivan Karp – combing, not galleries, but studios all the time, and that's what Barr... and Aldrich were relying on.'

This combination of circumstances led a number of distinguished collectors to buy Vern Blosum paintings within a brief period of time: the list included Betty and Leonard Asher of Los Angeles, Robert and Ethel Scull of New York, and G. David Thompson of Pittsburgh. The Blosum in the Thompson Collection has proven difficult to locate, as G. David, who bought the painting in 1964, only a year before he died, was inconsistent in his last wishes; one group of works was sold to the Kunstsammlung Nordrhein–Westfalen in Düsseldorf, while another was bequeathed to the Peru, Indiana, high school from which he graduated. Robert Scull kept his

Blosum painting, 'Twin Expiration' (1962), in the wake of his divorce from wife Ethel, and in 1981 donated it to the Weatherspoon Art Museum in Greensboro, North Carolina. Betty Asher took over the L. M. Asher Family Collection (including 'Twenty Five Minutes') after her husband Leonard lost interest in modern art and the two divorced. Betty did not mention Vern Blosum in her 1980 oral history interview for the Smithsonian's Archives of American Art; she passed away in 1994, so it will likely be impossible to know with any certainty how 'Twenty Five Minutes' went from her collection to a storage facility in Chatsworth.

Greg Allen draws a connection between the artist's rapid eclipse and his inadequate response to Alfred Barr's request for an autobiography. Having to ask such questions at all cast doubt on the seriousness of Blosum's enterprise, and this was a major transgression of unspoken rules of the museum. In his letter, Barr barely hides his annoyance, and he not only uses the word 'serious', but closes with 'Yours seriously'. He had chosen 'Time Expired' himself from Leo Castelli's back room, so to some extent his own reputation was at risk. At that time the Museum of Modern Art's position was simplicity itself: modern art of worth did not exist without an identifiable artist as creator. Blosum failed to present himself in person to any of the interested parties, and therefore seemed intent on throwing away what is conventionally known as a career. Allen summed up the situation bluntly, 'I would imagine that having Alfred Barr pissed at you and your work would be a blow for any artist's place in the history books.'

In his last writing about Blosum, posted on 9 September, 2011, Greg Allen made his most dramatic revelation: he had met the painter, seen his work, and interviewed him. He confirmed that 'Vern Blosum' was indeed a pseudonym invented by a living artist who was still painting and whose true identity he had promised not to reveal. Allen ended his blog's account with an (as yet) unfulfilled promise to tell the full story of Vern Blosum.

❡ At the end of 2011, I wrote the following for *ARTFORUM*:

> I discovered Vern Blosum's painting 'Twenty Five Minutes' in Cardwell Jimmerson's *SUB-POP*, an impeccably researched exhibition that sought to diminish the aura of historical inevitability surrounding the Pop Art canon. Blosum's early 1960s works ... suited their moment perfectly, but the identity of Blosum himself remains a secret ... Blosum executed a series of flatly rendered parking meters, perhaps as a hoax that succeeded too well to be sustained.

Constrained on one hand by the magazine's fact–checker, who obviously wished to stick to verifiable facts, and on the other hand by the sketchy information I had available to me, I was able to say almost nothing about a painting and an artist stranded somewhere beyond the reach of art history. Through Tom Jimmerson, I arranged an interview with the painter who worked as Vern Blosum. He agreed to speak with me, and I promised (as Greg Allen did) not to reveal his real name. Aside from this proviso, I was free to ask whatever question I wished about the artist and the pseudonym by which he is better known.

The man who called himself Vern Blosum was born in Elgin, Illinois in 1934. (The South Elgin address he supplied to the Museum of Modern Art was that of his parents' house.) His mother and father did not die when he was young; he invented this to introduce drama into the fictional life of the artist. He was far from self–taught, but had extensive formal training in art, beginning in high school. He graduated with a BFA in painting from the University of Denver.

After his undergraduate days, there was a period of travelling around the American West and trying his hand at various jobs. In response to the line of the Vern Blosum autobiography stating that his first job was running cars into Mexico for resale, he said,

> Well, I wouldn't want to admit that, but that's close to the truth. A friend of mine, who was a body and fender person, came from Oklahoma ... He was illiterate. He took a painting course from me, and he was just fantastic. The guy had skill – it was just unbelievable. We became very good friends, and we had a body shop ... I invested in that with him in California. You could take a car across the border into Mexico and sell it as a new re–built car and get a heck of a lot of money for it. That was back in the day, 1957, I think.

He also spent time in California selling cars – new ones, not used ones.

He studied briefly at UCLA with Adolph Gottlieb, who encouraged him to go to New York. He arrived there in 1959 and enrolled in a master's degree programme at Hunter College, where he concentrated on painting and taught undergraduate courses in lettering, life drawing, and art education. His primary interest was in abstract art. While he was a graduate student, he befriended David Smith and Richard Lippold, whom he helped with the installation of his sculpture 'Orpheus and Apollo' at Lincoln Center and replaced as a teacher during periods when Lippold was out of town. He spent time at the Cedar Tavern, where he met Mark Rothko and Robert Motherwell, both of whom he treated with deferential awe. 'I didn't say anything. I just listened. It was one hell of an experience.' In 1961, he had a solo exhibition of his abstract paintings at New York's Tibor de Nagy Gallery. The experience left him thoroughly disillusioned, and he then resolved to separate art and economics in his life. 'I adopted the [position I] still hold to this day: the painting has absolutely no value to me after I finish it. The value to me is in the process. I refuse to put a value on it, and I let other people do that. That keeps me removed from the whole concept of painting for money.' It was soon after this exhibition that he began painting under the name Vern Blosum.

He explained the origin of the name: 'I saw Mondrian's early work, paintings of flowers. Well, that sort of stuck in the back of my mind: vernal blossom. When I signed the back of the paintings, I would just put a 'V. Blosum', so many people called him Vern Blosum.' He began, logically enough, by making a series of flower paintings, and he applied himself to the task. 'It was very serious. The flowers were very sensitive, but the antithesis of what I did. I was a non–verbal painter, and the paintings were so obvious: flowers described by the botanical names underneath them.'

Painting realistically rendered common objects – flowers, and later, street furniture such as parking meters, mailboxes, public telephones, fire hydrants, and street signs – on blank backgrounds with redundant captions became the trademark Vern Blosum style. He made a total of forty–four paintings in this manner over four years. He divided his time between being an abstract painter five days a week and being Vern Blosum two days a week. During the whole period of Vern Blosum's activity, 1961 to 1964, he continued to teach, including a year as an instructor at Pratt Institute, which may have accounted for the rumour that 'Time Expired' was painted on a bet by a student there.

Despite the 'innuendos and indeed some flat statements' about Vern Blosum to which Barr referred in his letter, the man who made the paintings insists that only three other people knew his true identity: his parents and his girlfriend at the time. This woman, whom he preferred not to discuss at length, was his sole confederate in the Vern Blosum project. She acted as intermediary in consignments to Castelli and brought the paintings to Ivan Karp, the gallery director who had made his name by promoting and selling Pop Art.

Asked about what was happening in New York in the early 1960s, specifically the scene at Leo Castelli Gallery, the man who was once Vern Blosum said:

> My reaction to Pop Art was quite intense and quite aggravated. [Laughs] I thoroughly believed New York City was the centre of the art world at the time. Abstract painting was probably the first cultural event that we had seen in the US. That's the way it felt. So many things were happening. I was really involved and knew a lot of people – Lichtenstein and Warhol, of course, and I later did some things with Bob Rauschenberg. So I saw how this developed. They weren't Pop artists. Pop artists became them.
>
> The more I saw how the whole Pop Art scene began to develop, and having interacted with Ivan Karp at the Castelli Gallery ... I had no use for him, to be quite

E

> frank, because his approach to art was marketing, a Madison Avenue approach, which
> I knew first-hand ... I've been places where he would come to evaluate the art, in terms
> of whether he was interested in it and could sell it.

He saw the Pop artists as a group of individuals working independently, at first
unknown to each other, in a style that departed from the (avant-garde) mainstream
of abstract expressionism, and one that was much more marketable, whether this was
the intention of the artists or not. 'At the time, a lot of galleries and collectors realised,
we've got to find a new "ism". You know, what's the next thing to happen? I don't think
they found it as much as they built it. I should say they created it.'

Vern Blosum's paintings visualised the idea of limited time – in daily life and in
a mass culture changing ever more quickly – so well that Andy Warhol took notice
and delivered a version of his most famous utterance in the presence of one. 'Castelli
had my fifteen minute parking meter in his back room, and when Warhol saw it, he
said, "This is going to be his fifteen minutes of fame." It was so typical.' The story may
well be true, but if it isn't, it should be. Warhol would have seen the painting several
years before the aphorism 'In the future everyone will be world-famous for fifteen
minutes' appeared in print in the catalogue for his 1968 retrospective at the Moderna
Museet in Stockholm.

The man who made Vern Blosum's paintings had come to New York in the late
1950s in the hope of participating in the moment of abstract expressionism's glory,
only to discover that the moment those artists had spent decades working towards was
passing away. He was born too late; he arrived too late. He regularly encountered the
puzzled enthusiasm of the young:

> At the time, I was teaching all over the place, and I gave various lectures... this form
> of art [Pop] was taking over, but I never called it art. And I tried to explain what was
> happening. Every once in a while, a few of my good students would come up to me and
> say, "Wow, look at this. Who are these people threatening the art world with a bunch
> of crumpled papers in the corner of a room and calling it art?"

Artistic practice based upon formal technical training was definitively on its way
out of fashion, and the traditional artist's years of apprenticeship and searching were
replaced by what he denounced, in the tone of an instructor, as 'instant gratification'.

The early 1960s also saw the beginnings of a shift in the way the life's work of
an artist was perceived: from vocation to career. Previous generations of American
artists – up to and including some of the abstract expressionists – had no realistic hope
of making a living or achieving fame with their work, but in the space of a few years,
a market for modern art coalesced in New York, and providing art for that market was

a new figure: the professional artist. Inevitably, during this unprecedented economic boom, many conversations revolved around money, which had become an important, and non-aesthetic, standard of value for art.

> I'll never forget [when a friend] came running up to me and said, "I just sold this painting for X dollars. Wow, isn't that great?" And he showed me the cheque. You know, something's wrong here. I said, "Oh, great." I don't know ... I just was against money.

This abstractionist by choice and temperament reacted by hiding behind a new name, one he made up, and by painting in a style he didn't consider authentic, the one that was expected of him, until he gave up the Vern Blosum character in 1964.

> I didn't need to go any further. I felt that I had fulfilled all of my predictions. Even in '64, I sensed that there was a definite disinterest in Pop Art. The only thing that kept Pop Art alive was how the different gallery owners and investors built this stable, and through promotion, kept it going and kept the values high... you know, auction values. The whole financial end of it, how to get value out of this work, became almost a science.
>
> How did I react? I stopped painting. I did that both intellectually and figuratively, in the sense that I painted my stop sign. That was my last painting. That was the end. Why go on any further? Some of my friends were achieving success – they were overwhelmed with their success. What the hell does that have to do with painting? I was too much involved with learning my own identity through painting, rather than trying to paint an identity for somebody else to buy.

For several years he gave the market what it needed, and the response was positive. He had proven his point.

But there was a personal aspect to all of this as well, one he was reluctant to explain, concerning Vern Blosum's confederate, the woman with whom he lived for several years. In the greg.org obituary of Ivan Karp, Greg Allen quotes at length from the description of Leo Castelli Gallery in Karp's 1969 oral history interview for the Archives of American Art:

> "So kind of unknowingly the gallery by being what it was, an outgoing open place became a centre of activity. People come in here and spend a lot of time. They'd meet each other. Every Saturday was an important event at the gallery. Dozens of people standing around in the back room discovering each other ... What always made the gallery activity worthwhile for me was the number of beautiful people and especially the beautiful girls who always came in. They were always particularly welcome; as

E

they are today still. That's where I met my wife – at the gallery. She brought in slides and, in fact, brought in some paintings of an artist she was interested in. And I guess I was more interested in her than I was in the painter. But I think we did show the artist. And then I married his sponsor."

This painter was Vern Blosum. When I met Blosum almost fifty years later, it was clear he remembered the sting of losing his girlfriend as if it was yesterday.... When I called Ivan several years ago out of the blue and told him I wanted to talk with him about Vern Blosum, he just laughed and laughed.

The 'innuendos and indeed some flat statements' about a phony painter that so troubled Alfred Barr undoubtedly had their origin in the pillow talk of Mr and soon-to-be Mrs Karp.

Seeing the beginnings of an art scene where each 'new ism' declares its predecessors deadly dull or irrelevant and discovering that his girlfriend preferred to be with one of the men responsible for creating this environment, the artist known as Vern Blosum must have become deeply embittered. He reacted by leaving town and pursuing a Ph.D. in Art Education at the University of Massachusetts. As a professional academic rather than a professional artist, he continued to paint, but he did so during his vacations and in a style no longer fashionable.

He could be dismissed as a has-been (or a never-was) who played a prank to confirm his worst suspicions about those around him, and thus feel superior to them. But while interviewing him, I suggested other ways to think about Vern Blosum. Though this 'non-verbal' painter wouldn't have used the same words I did, he patiently listened to my characterisation of his pseudonymous practice:

> You could describe Vern Blosum, not as a joke or a hoax, but as a philosophical proposition. He embodied certain ideas about the work of art at a specific moment in history, and because of this he was embraced. He was a kind of test case. You put forth a hypothesis about the art world taking shape, and it was confirmed by the success of Vern Blosum's paintings ... The use of a pseudonym is the great distinction of this practice. There are recent artists who have obscured their identities somewhat by working collectively or under pseudonyms, but in fact, these people are rather famous; they circulate in the world under their real names and have careers. What interests me is how disciplined you were in maintaining your secret identity. It's the stuff of comic books, like *SUPERMAN* ... Pseudonyms are quite common in literature. Writers have a lot of reasons to hide their names – political, aesthetic, or financial – but this is extremely uncommon in modern art. As far as I've been able to determine, yours is a unique case of someone making successful work under an assumed name and not taking credit for it or exploiting the situation. Your practice leads us to consider certain

problems with the way art history is written, the way museums function, and the way the art market operates.

Vern Blosum's response to all of this was, 'Whoa, you just hit the nail on the head there. I completely agree with you.' The terms I used may have been anachronistic, and the results of his work may have borne only a slight relation to his original intentions; indeed, there may have been an element of opportunism in his agreement with me. Nonetheless, my account can serve as an explanation of why contemporary spectators are fascinated by the reappearance of these paintings that look like Pop Art.

¶ At the moment when MOCA, Los Angeles' most troubled major cultural institution, gave over two of its buildings to Urs Fischer, whose work – wasteful and luxurious yet hideously ugly 'bad boy' art produced by alienated means of production – is the very quintessence of the contemporary circa 2013, the museum's director, Jeffrey Deitch, saw the work of Vern Blosum at an artist-run alternative space in Culver City. After taking it all in while displaying his best poker face, Deitch expressed an interest in buying the very last Blosum, 'Stop' (1964), 'assuming all provenance questions can be answered to his satisfaction', as his associate put it delicately. When he was being driven away, he asked somewhat less delicately, 'Who's to say the artists in that room aren't themselves the painters behind those paintings?' He could have taken the words right out of the mouth of Alfred H. Barr, Jr. fifty years previously. In the realm of literary criticism, Roland Barthes announced the 'death of the author' in 1967, yet art's authors continue to play the most protracted death scene ever staged. In fact, most comprehensive museums are full of 'authorless' art, from ancient and medieval times, or from what we condescendingly call the Third World, indigenous populations and 'outsider' artists whose proper names we may never know. The real innovation of the modern is the extremity of individualism, as the promoters of art in a capitalist economy perpetually need artists to single out, to lionise, to blame, to forget then rediscover. The figure of the artist is the last modernist myth to survive the successive waves of earnest critique and cynical iconoclasm in this overreaching, globalised art industry.

∴

¶ I wrote the essay 'Vern Blosum, Phantom' for a booklet published by Assembly, a collective of artists who presented an exhibition of paintings by Blosum. While the show was on view, an editor of a contemporary art website approached Assembly and asked for permission to post my essay online. I was sceptical, since this website had not been known to provide any kind of forum for critical reflection about art. In the interest of bringing timely publicity to what I considered a worthwhile project, I set aside my doubts and consented to the website's request, on the condition that my essay would appear without editorial changes.

'Vern Blosum, Phantom' was posted on 30 September, 2013, and remained online for several hours. By the time I attempted to get access to the essay the next day, the link to it was dead. I had had no direct contact with the website's editors, so I asked Assembly to make an inquiry.

On 2 October, the following message was forwarded to me:

> We ended up removing William's essay from the site because Vern Blosum
> has some issues with it being disseminated. As he and the gallery work things
> out, we decided to defer to his wishes in the meantime.

The next day, I received another message:

> Thanks for your note. We took the link down at the request of the artist … In
> general, our policy has been to defer to the will of the artist when issues come
> up. Since we don't have the chance to see every exhibition in person or know
> the full story behind every show, we feel it's appropriate to follow the artist's
> decision about what best represents the work.

I received further communications that mentioned Vern's discomfort with my mention of his relationship with the woman who later married Ivan Karp and my use of the phrase 'pillow talk' in reference to them.

While I can sympathise with a man still wounded by a fifty-year-old rejection, I hold that a matter of principle is at stake. I have two main objections to the explanations offered to me. First, art historians and critics should not depend upon any artist's permission to publish their work. When they (and those who publish them) defer to artists' wishes, they risk surrendering their independence and writing what amounts to advertising copy. I was not commissioned to write an advertisement, nor did I receive a fee. Second, the statements about Vern's personal life were not based upon confidences disclosed during my interview with him, but upon what I found in Ivan Karp's oral history interview for the Smithsonian's Archives of American Art and in the contents of greg.org. Anyone with access to the internet and an interest in these questions could have reached the same conclusions I did. An artist has the right to ask for a correction or retraction in cases of factual error, but this right does not extend to suppressing an essay because it hurt his feelings.

¶ In the aftermath of my essay's brief appearance, I quickly realised that something more than feelings were at issue; I had been deceived. I regretted that I had not questioned more thoroughly Vern Blosum's eager assent to my more tendentious claims about the importance of his pseudonymous practice. I later found out that the editor of the art website to which I had sent the essay was a personal friend of a commercial gallerist who had been manoeuvring to gain control of Vern Blosum's body of work, and that the request to suppress the text came from him and not from the artist himself. Furthermore, this gallerist had initiated legal proceedings against the gallery that mounted the original Vern Blosum exhibition and commissioned my essay.

In its perverse complexities, this affair reminded me of the worldly fortunes of Giorgio de Chirico (1888–1978). He did not work under an assumed name, but he did spend the greater part of his life pursuing unfashionable artistic goals in the face of general indifference. From 1909 to 1918, de Chirico made the paintings for which he is best known: views of deserted piazzas, fragments of the classical past juxtaposed with common objects enlarged in scale, and distant trains passing forlorn houses in an unidentified Mediterranean city. Drawn to the arcades of Turin – the city of Nietzsche, the philosopher de Chirico read most avidly – the pioneer of metaphysical painting imbued his cityscapes with a sense of the uncanny that inspired the Surrealists years later.

After an initial period of extensive exhibition and critical praise, de Chirico turned against these paintings. He publicly stated his opposition to modern art, an opposition he maintained for the remaining sixty years of his life. In his essay 'The Return of Craftsmanship' (1919), he declared his intention to adopt a traditional painting technique to rival the old masters, but in his writing he continued to employ a style reminiscent of the metaphysical paintings, most successfully in his astonishing and unique novel, *HEBDOMEROS* (1929). His traditionalist position would become completely entrenched a decade later, when he began to paint in a style he called neo–baroque. By the exalted standards de Chirico set for his late paintings, they are certainly failures, yet they contain something sublime that escapes his explicit intentions. Particularly remarkable – or hideous, depending on one's point of view – is 'Self Portrait in a Park' (1959), which looks like Gainsborough's 'Blue Boy' re-imagined in red by a slightly pudgy and very serious elderly transvestite. Wide (though not universal) appreciation for such work came only after de Chirico's death, with postmodernism's embrace of classical references, pastiche, and 'bad painting'.

Life for de Chirico after the age of 30 must have been a refinement of torture. By the time he reaped the benefits of fame, he had dismissed his celebrated works as belonging to an 'immature' past, while at the same time, almost no one would pay attention to the works he really cared about and painted in great number. He also

E

came to understand that the profit potential of a small body of historical work was limited, especially since many of the best pictures had already been sold. He became bitter, and in his bitterness became vengeful towards an art market that did not value his later works as highly as he did. He regularly denounced de Chirico paintings in important collections as forgeries, and to add to the confusion, he introduced back-dated 'self-forgeries' onto the market. He would approach a dealer with a recently-painted work bearing a date falling between 1909 and 1918 and executed in his characteristic metaphysical style, and explain that he had found the painting under his bed. This happened so often that dealers began to joke that de Chirico's bed was six feet off the floor.

¶ There was an element of folly in my ambition to write a strictly factual account of an artistic practice based upon an imposture. I suspect it was exactly my adherence to the facts that those who stood to profit most from Vern Blosum's paintings found objectionable; publicity that allowed room for invention would have been much more useful. By exerting control over the discourse around these paintings, Vern Blosum's dealer attempted to will them from a state of obscurity to commercial exploitation with no period of public appreciation or critical commentary in between. Without this context, a 'Vern Blosum' can be whatever a dealer or collector wishes it to be, painted by anyone at any time in any number of variations, and the corpus can expand from forty-four attested historical works to whatever number the market will bear. Consequently, I have come to see virtue in Alfred Barr's position on the question of an artwork's authenticity. I still believe a critique of authorship in art is necessary, but I think in my eagerness to find an embodiment of this critique, I was drawn unwittingly into a confidence game.

E

# XI

# INTERVIEW

## WITH

# JACQUES RANCIÈRE

JACQUES RANCIÈRE CAME TO PROMINENCE in 1968 when, under the auspices of his teacher Louis Althusser, he contributed to the seminal volume READING CAPITAL. In 1974 Rancière published his first book, ALTHUSSER'S LESSON, a historical analysis of the French Left in the 1960s and 1970s, in which he critiqued his teacher's structural Marxism and his denunciation of the May '68 student uprisings. Rejecting the Maoist philosophies that inflected these events, Althusser refused to support the students on the grounds that their rebellion was not led by the Parti communiste français. In his book Rancière relates this to the 'return to order' that followed these tumultuous times.

Rancière's main political idea is that a democratic politics emerges from the presupposition of equality. Equality is a starting point, not a goal or destination. This idea is articulated to various degrees in all of Rancière's books. It finds its most polemical expression in DISAGREEMENT: POLITICS AND PHILOSOPHY, published in 1998, though it is argued with equal force in the lesser-known book THE IGNORANT SCHOOLMASTER, where Rancière considers the pedagogical ideas of the post-revolutionary philosopher of education Joseph Jacotot. More recently his work has turned to the relation between aesthetics and politics. In texts such as THE POLITICS OF AESTHETICS and THE FUTURE OF THE IMAGE, Rancière attempts to shift the parameters of criticism away from traditional forms of critique which, in their tendency to demystify, situate the critic in a position of authority in relation to his or her object. His latest book, AISTHESIS, attempts to reimagine aesthetic experience as a fundamentally democratic process that is accessible to all.

This interview took place in Rancière's hotel room on the Gray's Inn Road in North London. The room was cramped and unadorned, the paint was peeling off the bare walls in large swaths, and there was only one chair, so that Rancière was forced to sit on his unmade bed. He spoke quickly and nervously, his words barely able to keep up with the movements of his thought.

———————

Q. THE WHITE REVIEW — It would be helpful if you could begin by defining the relationship between your central political idea and your current work on aesthetics.

A. JACQUES RANCIÈRE — My starting point when dealing with aesthetics was a polemical one. I took a polemical stance in relation to a certain way of framing what modernity is and what modern art is. I wanted to rethink the very notion of the aesthetic.

When I started work on the subject there was a very influential book, LA DISTINCTION [1979], by French sociologist Pierre Bourdieu, which put forward the idea that aesthetic judgement had always been determined by a

dominant class which defined aesthetic concepts such as taste. In other words, there was a disjunction between the aesthetic and the popular. But I felt the contrary might be the case. At first the idea of aesthetic judgement had an egalitarian capacity. What is important in Immanuel Kant's idea of aesthetic judgement – of judgement without a concept – and what is entailed in Friedrich Schiller's idea of the aesthetic education of man, is that the capacity for aesthetic judgement does not belong to a particular class or group of people but is a capacity that is widely shared. That is the first point.

The second point is that, against the

so-called modernist tradition, where you find a distinction between high art and popular art, autonomous art and everyday experience, it seemed to me that what we really find in the history of modern art, or what I call the 'aesthetic regime of art', is a blurring of the boundaries between the artistic and the non-artistic.

Q. THE WHITE REVIEW — In relation to your last point, you conceive of the modernist tradition as a new aesthetic regime of art, but at the same time you have insisted that it is not just an artistic development but an indication of wider social and political changes, or, as you sometimes put it, a 'reconfiguration of the distribution of the sensible'. Yet in your writings on art and aesthetics, and in each 'scene' of your recently translated book *Aisthesis*, you focus on a particular work of art, performance, or what you call a 'singular sensible event', while the broader social and political changes are held at bay. Could you elaborate on the implications of this methodology in relation to the polemical stance you have taken?

A. JACQUES RANCIÈRE — Each 'scene' in *Aisthesis* attempts to do away with the usual way of doing theory. That is to say, of adopting an overarching view which seeks to unify under a single concept a multiplicity of empirical events. This is an approach I do not find productive. What are important for me are the reflections on a work of art and the attempts to construct a sensible world for that 'event'. There is no work of art in front of you, as such, but there is always a transference from the visual to the verbal, a transference which creates the very possibility of the work becoming a sensible event. What is important about the 'scene' is that you are no longer the theorist looking at the empirical world from above. Instead, it is the art object which teaches you

how to look at it and how to talk and think about it.

This is related to my former writing on workers' emancipation. I attempted in that to avoid the usual empirical approach, in which a narrative is produced about the struggles of workers which becomes the object of theory. Instead I looked at the narratives produced by workers and considered them as being in some way already theoretical. Producing these narratives was a way for workers to take a view of their own lives and to reconstruct their own lives. They constitute an attempt to emphasise, rephrase and translate an experience, to grasp the very flesh of experience. Likewise, the purpose of the 'scene' is to focus on the construction of a network, the construction of modes of perception and forms of intelligibility that transform an object or performance into a sensible event called art.

Q. THE WHITE REVIEW — But you nevertheless extract something from that singularity which appears to be universal. You start with a single art object or performance, or the reception of a particular work but, whether you are writing about the Victorian dramatist Edward Gordon Craig or James Agee's response to a photograph by Walker Evans, you end up drawing similar conclusions. These conclusions tend to revolve around notions of inaction, what you refer to variously as the 'radical logic of inaction', of 'suspended action', of 'indifference', of 'leaving things undone'. It sometimes comes across as an ethic of depersonalisation, a will-to-nothing. Could you elaborate on this?

A. JACQUES RANCIÈRE — Well, it's a big issue. What I think was at the core of the aesthetic revolution in the nineteenth century was a rupture of the dominant model of rationality, which hinged on the cause/effect relation. This was connected to the classical, organic model of the work of art, which imagined the work as a totality, with its head, its members, its proportions, etc.

What I saw as a basic feature of the aesthetic regime is a break with that organic and hierarchical model. For me it starts with the German art historian Johann Joachim Winckelmann, who wrote about the 'Torso del Belvedere', a mutilated statue of Hercules with no head or limbs. It is a work that cannot be judged with respect to ideas of organicity and perfection. It is deprived of all the elements which might decide and anticipate the effects of its viewing. Yet for Winckelmann it was the epitome of Greek beauty. So the disruption of the organic model also disrupts the causal chain, and with it nineteenth-century models of rationality, or perhaps modern rationality more generally. Such a work disrupts the view of art as a totality that you can grasp in its infrastructure and in its effects. The causal relation is interrupted.

There is something here that is comparable to the experience of suspension, inaction, or reverie. And all this forms an important part of that emblematic image of the worker who stops the labour of his hand in order to look out through the window and take an aesthetic view from the place in which he works. There is also a relation here to nineteenth-century literature, which attempted to produce a total picture of society, but whose plots often lead nowhere. In a sense they are about the failure of action.

Q. THE WHITE REVIEW — And this leads you to imagine inaction as activity? Could this be associated with the strike perhaps?

A. JACQUES RANCIÈRE — Precisely. There are two moments that are important in the history of workers' struggles. Firstly, the moment when the strike is invented: not only as

a reaction but also as a demonstration of rationality and of the integral capacity of the worker. The second moment has to do with moving away from the strike as a way of obtaining an advantage in a conflict towards the strike as a general stop, a way of getting out of the game. The general strike is really the peak of the struggle and a way of moving aside. Inaction precisely being something extracted from the old couples passivity/activity; recreation/leisure. There is something active to inaction, because it allows you to get out of the system. You find this in Stendhal's novel THE RED AND THE BLACK, where the protagonist discovers in prison that inaction is a destiny which is both more desirable and more inaccessible for the plebeian than reaching the top of society.

Q. THE WHITE REVIEW — Do you see inaction as an aesthetic gesture, a fusion of art and life, a 'becoming-art', to use your own term?

A. JACQUES RANCIÈRE — What is important for me is the moment when aesthetic experience becomes a form of experience that reveals a universal human capacity, as it does in the image of the worker gazing out of the window. It is a capacity that can be found everywhere, in everyday life, in the streets, in a glance. Think of Baudelaire's prose poems: in the public gardens the eyes of the poor look at the splendours of the café. Then there is Emma Bovary, who wishes to put art in life and to find art in life. And there were also the programmes of the Soviet revolution, the dream of art becoming life and of life becoming art, the dream of constructing the forms of a new life. What is interesting to me is that all this was not only an intellectual programme. It sought to transform the tissue of lived experience.

Q. THE WHITE REVIEW — In relation to

literature, Alain Badiou has claimed that your work inhabits the interval between documentary and fiction. What place does fiction hold in your work, not so much the fictions you write about but the fictions you produce? When I read your work I am always struck by its style, its lyricism. You often write lyric inventories that have a certain poetry or rhythm to them. What does it mean for you to write in this way? How does the sensible fabric of your writing bear on your understanding of the relation between narrative discourse and historical representation, philosophy and its object?

A. JACQUES RANCIÈRE —— The ground for this is to question the very opposition between theory and narration, between philosophy and other forms of discourse. It ties up with the idea that theory is poetry, that theory is fiction. Not because fiction has to do with the invention of imaginary worlds but because fiction is an attempt to tie words with action and words with images. Philosophical discourse is also a form of fiction. It is an attempt to reconstruct the relation between signifieds and signifiers, and that is fiction. So I attempt to create a level of equality between discourses that are normally thought of in hierarchical terms. That is the first point.

The second point is that I am somebody who really likes to look at images, to spend time in front of them, and I am someone who likes words. For me it is very important to try to grasp the sensible texture of a discourse, a discourse which has tried to reproduce the sensible texture of an event or performance. This is something I try to do myself. There is also the idea that you must read and reread a text. Not only to understand what it is about but to discover what kind of sensible texture or intellectual energy inhabits it. It's a way of getting out of the immediate perception of

meaning in order to ask: What sensible world does the work construct?

Q. THE WHITE REVIEW —— So you try to allow your words to inhabit the works in question?

A. JACQUES RANCIÈRE —— Yes. But it also has to do with the reader. There is always this pressure to be clear, to be at the supposed level of the reader or spectator, for everything to be explicit. And of course there is the analytic tradition of philosophy, according to which every word must be transparent. Well, no. There is something human to the fact that words are not transparent, that words cannot be exhausted by signification. With words and sentences there is always something more that you must read and then read again. People need to find their own ways in your text, paths that are not already drawn. This ties up with intellectual emancipation. We must really get rid of this obsession with understanding, this idea that you have to understand, that things must be made understandable. Transparency is a form of interdiction, a form of prohibition.

Q. THE WHITE REVIEW —— Is this opacity related to your rejection of the figure of the knowing critic, who is supposed to dispel myths and unveil truths? I ask because in a somewhat crude article ['Post-Critical', OCTOBER issue 139] the art historian Hal Foster rejected your methods in favour of a more traditional form of critique, the kind that is normally associated with writers like Theodor W. Adorno, Walter Benjamin and other members of the Frankfurt School, which ultimately takes the form of a critique of capital and its dynamics. Could you unpack the relation between this mode of critique and your own discourse? I'm thinking also of your claim that 'critical art' intervenes only because of the lack of politics in the proper sense.

A. JACQUES RANCIÈRE —— Well, critique means

many things. In certain traditions a critic is a person who knows the rules for making good art: 'This is good art because it follows such and such a rule.' For me the function of the critic today is different. It is not to say that this is good or bad art, but to ask what made it possible or impossible for such an object or performance to be understood as art. The task of the critic is to try to reconstruct the world in which a sensible event is understood as art, whether it be popular pantomime or the Romantic notion of art for art's sake. This, for me, is the function of the art or literary critic.

Today one also finds the idea that the art critic is an intellectual who critiques society, meaning of course revealing the truth behind false appearances. This tradition of critique, the critique of society, of images, of spectacle, and so-called 'critical art' more generally, is related to the critical function of unveiling truths and of provoking awareness and energy. Today this form of critique has become a nihilistic discourse which claims that all people are idiots enthralled by the spectacle, that people take pleasure in their own humiliation, etc. It argues that the forces of the market and market consumption are everywhere, that everything has become a commodity, that even protests have become commodities. The fact is that this critical tradition has produced the very thing it set out to critique! So I'm trying to be critical of the critical tradition. You can say that this means 'anything goes', that there are no criteria, and so on. You can say that this is relativism. I would simply say that, today, I don't know what could be the criteria that would allow one to relate sensible events or works of art to the truth of the system.

Q. THE WHITE REVIEW —— How then do you account for the close relationship between the work of art and the commodity fetish?

A. JACQUES RANCIÈRE —— Look, we all know that art belongs to a market system. The very idea of the commodity as a fetish is problematic. It rests on the idea that the power of a system is exercised through its own dissimulation and that this dissimulation takes on the form of a religious relation to an object of worship. From that point on it is easy to equate aesthetic distance to a religious attitude denying the commodity nature of the artwork. This form of 'Marxism' is exactly the one Marx laughs at in THE GERMAN IDEOLOGY: finding religion everywhere in order to establish oneself in the position of demystifier. I thought it more interesting to analyse the contradictory purposes and requirements that shaped the museum form of exhibition of the artworks and the type of gaze that it elicited. Moreover it is clear that the power of the market today is disconnected from any form of worship of the art work. Saatchi or Pinault's collections don't appeal to any kind of sacralisation of the artwork; they simply bear witness to the social importance of their owners. They hide nothing. On the contrary: they make the power of capitalism still more visible.

In addition, the idea of fetishism is divided in two, but the connection between these two aspects is not at all obvious. On the one hand there is the idea of the icon, which is something sacred. On the other hand there is the idea of something that hides something else. The idea that criticising the fetish and its autonomy means restoring things to their truth, which is invariably the truth of the market, involves mixing two very different things together.

The autonomy of the artwork or performance is opposed to the idea of the fetish. It is not about looking at a work from a distance but of inhabiting that work. The idea of a theatre for everybody, as found in the writings of the stage designer Adolphe Appia, is really the idea of a theatre without a spectator. I would oppose that to the tradition that imagines the spectacle to be something purely negative, an idea which can be traced back to Plato. For me, this fusion of art and life has nothing to do with the fetish.

Q. THE WHITE REVIEW —— In the final pages of *AISTHESIS* you write of 'an art attuned to all the vibrations of universal life: an art capable both of matching the accelerated rhythms of industry, society and urban life, and of giving infinite resonance to the most ordinary minutes of everyday life'. Is such an art possible today?

A. JACQUES RANCIÈRE —— Perhaps this question can be tied to the preceding one. I should say that this passage does not necessarily transcribe my own utopian dream. But it ties up with many artistic traditions, from futurism to Whitman's dream of a world that becomes poetical as you are passing by, a world where everything gravitates around the words of the poet. Think also of all those dreams that hinged on the relation between art and electricity, and ideas of universal communication. The point is that this kind of unanimist or simultaneist dream of art condensing universal life has many possibilities that are ignored by the so-called critical or modernist tradition. The upsetting of the relation between high and low culture that occurred in the 1960s, for instance, is really quite reductive in relation to that poetics. The operations involved in Warhol's 'Campbell's Soup Cans' or his 'Brillo Boxes', for example, were supposed to function as provocations. But I think that those forms of provocation reduce the possibility of art participating in universal life to an affirmation of the identity of art and the commodity form. That is also what I think about those

who hang so much on Marcel Duchamp and the readymade. Because Duchamp's time was also the time of Bauhaus, a time when people tried to put art into every object of everyday life. For me this is much more interesting than the logic of the readymade.

When I wrote the passage you cited I was thinking of James Agee and the way he describes the inside of the house and the decorum of impoverished sharecroppers. He tries to introduce universal life into the details he relates. Which means that he tries to capture the universal in the sharecropper's house, in the sleep of the sharecroppers, in the atmosphere and in the night. In a way he tried to find a cosmic dimension to all of these details. What I wanted to emphasise is that, if modern art means something, it means the dream of an art which can resonate with universal life, an art which offers a way of linking the singularity of a sensible event with the vibrations of the universal.

RYE DAG HOLMBOE, JUNE 2013

# RESISTANCE

BY

# CHRIS KRAUS

31 Standish Ave.,
Rosedale, Toronto 5
7 February, 1963


Dear Mr and Mrs Tuck, -

Thank you for your nice Christmas card which arrived well before Christmas. I
wish you could have seen the seventy-two cards I had on display in our living
room, and among them was the one from you. Christmas is a busy time, but
interesting. My Christmas Day was a lonely one until I left the house at 4:30
in the afternoon to go downtown to have my supper in a restaurant. Following
that, I went to my cousin's home to spend the evening. I was back home at 11
o'clock, and was soon off to bed. However, there was one 'bright spot' while
I was alone - it was Her Majesty's Christmas Message. I'm sure you heard it too.
    I was glad to get your letter early in December, and to know the calendar
arrived safely. You said you had not been well, but was feeling better. You also
said that Mrs. Tuck had high blood pressure, and was not feeling well. I do
hope she is much improved. Do take good care of yourselves — both of you. Good
health is our greatest asset.
    I do part-time work, so keep plenty busy. This house seems to require quite
a lot of my time. In a house there is always something requiring to be done,
and I do all my own work. Even though I live alone, I find plenty to do. It is
quite a responsibility, as well as expense, but I have to live somewhere, and
apartments, too, are expensive. I much prefer one's own home, to an apartment,
so I will carry on here as long as I can do so.
    I think I told you that John and his wife were going to California for
Christmas. John enjoyed himself, and said the time was too short.
    We have had a good share of cold weather, but as yet not much snow. Winter
is getting by, and we will all welcome spring. Can you notice the daylight
stretching out? It is quite noticeable here, and I always watch this with
interest.
    You said you and Mrs Tuck would see what this coming summer would bring
forth, and perhaps you could both make a trip up here. That would be very nice,
and this home will make you welcome, should you wish to stay here — will cost
you nothing. You will not see Mother, but I will take care of you both as best
I can.
    This is all for this time. Write when you can. Your letters are welcome.


                                        Sincerely,
                                        Bertha Lowe

¶ I found this letter in a disused Anglican school building in Pouch Cove, a town fifteen miles north of St John's, Newfoundland. The letter was typed and tacked onto a board in one of the bathrooms. In its last incarnation, the school had been used by a foundation to house visiting artists from all over the world. One of the artists must have scavenged it out of the pile of debris in the mouldering building, which had been red-tagged last summer during a drawn-out dispute between the foundation director and the Pouch Cove Building and Safety Department. The letter was touching in its archaism. Beyond its literal obsolescence – who, who isn't trying to be quaint or cute, writes letters anymore? – it reflected certain lost cultural values: an absence of high expectations, a stoic acceptance of loneliness. It reminded me of my parents. I copied it into my notebook.

¶ During the past several years I've chosen to live somewhat nomadically, accepting various invitations from cultural institutions like the one in Pouch Cove. I have a house that I'm rarely in near downtown Los Angeles. The house has a value – although not to me, since I'm usually travelling – so I often loan it to friends, friends-of-friends, family members, even passing acquaintances met during these travels. (During the past several years I've noticed the fierce desire that once pre-empted rational choice evaporating. Slightly confused, I concluded the best course to follow was: if I don't actively want something and someone else does, just let them have it. This applied to my house.)

Last August, when I arrived at the house in LA en route to Pouch Cove after spending the summer in Mexico, I noticed several small, insignificant things misplaced or missing. The front door key (redundant, since I leave the house open) was gone; also, the TV remote and the black plastic scoop used to measure expresso-ground coffee. I asked Justin and Karen and Bob and Jerome and Rose and Samantha and Joan – all of whom used the place briefly during my absence – about these things, but no one knew anything. Nothing major was missing and the house was left clean. There was no one to blame, certainly nothing to rage about – but the losses were very unsettling. Each of these things was part of my LA routine, which, I liked to think, resembled the life of a Seventies sitcom air hostess.

What bothered me most was the loss of the black plastic scoop. Made of hard shiny plastic, it came with the Bodum French Press-style coffee pot sold at Starbucks for $34.95. I'd encountered a similar problem two years ago, when houseguests Charlie and Billy and Jane accidentally broke the glass flask. They left a nice note and ten dollars. Theoretically the flask was replaceable for $10.95, but the Silverlake Starbucks (a thirty-minute round trip from my house) was out of stock on this item. Faced with the choice of driving to Glendale, Pasadena or Burbank on one of my three days back in LA in the hope that one of those stores would have the

replacement, or simply buying the whole thing again, I surrendered my credit card…
though not without airing my views on softly-enforced consumption to the barista; a
rant as wasted as the use of air-quotes around phrases like 'choose to service my own
account' to call centre workers in prison, or India.

But the 'challenges' posed by the loss of the black plastic scoop during the summer
proved insurmountable. (I'd just 'concluded' six months of therapy, after concluding
that the seventy-five minute round trip drive to an inconvenient Westside location
to discuss my resistance just wasn't worth it. It occurs to me now, as I think of the
black plastic scoop, this fact might be relevant.) Because the black plastic scoop had
never been sold as a separate component of the Bodum French Press, at Starbucks
or anywhere, and moreover I learned, after driving to the Silverlake Starbucks, the
entire chain has stopped selling these coffee pots, replaced them with travel mugs.

Where do you find a black plastic scoop? I tried searching the web, but no luck.
Jerome, my ex-husband, was empathetic. (He and his girlfriend Rose were among
those using the house.) 'I am aware of the plastic scoop and its fragile existence,'
he said. This show of support nearly moved me to tears. Jerome understood. And
I wondered: just how much time and care should a person spend in the attempt to
replace a fetishised object? Or rather – a commonplace object that, in its absence and
newly unattainable state, becomes fetishised? Although Jerome was helpfully quick
to point out that this desire, transferred onto an object, in fact defines the term 'fetish'.
But was this correct? There was no Freudian guesswork involved in my need for
the black plastic scoop, no magical thinking. I'd already had a black plastic scoop. I
simply wanted it back.

Still, at a certain point, one must ask: At what point is it better to devote one's
mental focus to simply getting over the plastic scoop, and, as they say, 'moving on'?
Asking yourself this question is like asking what's real. Can you notice the daylight
stretching out? How do we accommodate loss, how do we live alongside it?

¶ When Walter Benjamin travelled to Moscow in the winter of 1926, he kept a
diary. He was not a habitual diarist. He was funding the trip by writing articles
for magazines back in Berlin, and took notes to make his job easier. He travelled
to Moscow because he wanted to see for himself what life in a realised communist
culture was like. He also travelled to Moscow because he wanted to see a woman he
loved, Asja Lācis.

He and Lācis had met two years before in Capri. At that time, he was married
and she already had two other lovers, but they embarked on an intellectual/erotic
romance which included the writing of manifestos and, presumably, some kind of
sexual congress. They met up in Berlin the next year, and then once again, in Riga.
Lācis, a Lithuanian actress, lived in Moscow with her companion, the theatre director

Bernhard Reich. She was a communist; a colleague of Meyerhold, Brecht. In Berlin, a few months before, Benjamin wrote: 'This street is named Asja Lācis Street, who laid it through the author,' a pretty sexual dedication to ONE WAY STREET, the book he'd just finished.

When Benjamin arrived in Moscow, Lācis was hospitalised in a sanatorium with a mysterious illness. Presumably Benjamin knew of her attachment to Reich; in fact, he found Reich 'a fabulous guy', and during his trip, the three spent most of their evenings together... at Asja's bedside playing dominoes and eating halvah; attending concerts and plays; meeting most of Moscow's cultural innovators. Sometimes Benjamin goes out alone with Reich. Sometimes Benjamin goes out with Asja, although he laments that they're 'rarely alone'.

What's astonishing about Benjamin's MOSCOW DIARY is that while his longing for Lācis pulses through his descriptions of Moscow, it does not overwhelm them. The trip is not about their doomed love; doomed love doesn't even necessarily inform all of his Moscow experience. The diary is a portrait of the most enviable, ultimate form of urbanity where grief exists and can be sampled, like some exquisitely potent local intoxicant. On 15 December he records that Lācis 'never turned up' for their date... and goes on to describe St Basil's Cathedral, Moscow arcades, wooden toys, the political histories of some acquaintances, and the 'beautiful view of the long string of lights' on Tverskoi Boulevard.

On New Year's Eve, the snow 'had the sparkle of stars ... When we arrived in front of her house, I asked her, more out of defiance and more to test her than out of any real feeling, for one last kiss in the old year. She wouldn't give me one. I turned back, it was now almost New Year's, certainly alone but not all that sad. After all, I knew that Asja, too, was alone.'

Benjamin's closest friend Gershom Scholem was not buying any of it. 'The diary is desperate in its outright urgency ... [it] leaves us without insight into or understanding of this intellectual dimension of the woman he loved ... The times he waits in vain for Asja, her continual rejections, and finally even the erotic cynicism that she displays to no uncertain extent ... makes the absence of any convincing evocation of her intellectual profile doubly enigmatic ... Everybody was bewildered by these two lovers who did nothing but quarrel.' And: 'the theme of their relationship', Gary Smith writes in the afterword, 'drawn as an erotic red thread ... is one of obsession and denial'. Harvard University Press reduces this further on their back–jacket copy to 'the account of his masochistic love affair with this elusive – and rather unsympathetic – object of desire.'

These interpretations of Benjamin's experience – clearly stated by him, in his own words, in his own diary – remind me of psychotherapy.

At the end of his trip, Benjamin lost sight of Lācis as his sleigh left the hotel, and

F

rode to the train station in tears. Nine years later, Bernhard Reich – together with all Jewish German émigrés – was banished from Moscow, then jailed. Lācis was interned for more than a decade in Kazakhstan, after the first Stalinist purge.

Who defines happiness? And is it a goal? We have had a good share of cold weather, but as yet not much snow. Is my need to recover the black plastic scoop masochistic, or is it more like – 'I know what I want' – a self-affirmation?

This is all for this time. Write when you can. Your letters are welcome.

# SELF-PORTRAIT WITH DE CHIRICO AND OTHER WORKS

BY

# JOSHUA ABELOW

# MR FRANKLIN D. HUFF

BY

# NICOLA BARKER

I DON'T KNOW WHY I imagined I'd make it all the way around to Hastings before the tide came in. It was an ambitious scheme, at best — not so much even a scheme as a blithe notion, a vague 'urge', a complete spur of the moment thing — and I was (quite frankly) unsuitably shod. It's a challenging walk, much of it demanding — with the tide coming in, out of sheer necessity — a measure of energetic clambering and even leaping from large rock to large rock.

An ambitious scheme, as I've said. A foolish scheme. And then, when I finally made it back (Forty-eight hours later! Barely still in possession of life and limb)... On my eventual return... The conquering hero (ha, ha, ha)...
*Urgh!* How else can I describe the vileness I encountered? Just... just... just plain... *urgh!*

Yes. *Yes.* So it *was* a rather silly plan, in retrospect. Irresponsible. I am currently in possession of the Tide Tables for Dungeness, Rye Bay and Hastings (courtesy of our Ms Hahn, no less; part of the cottage's 'Welcome Pack'). Pett Level doesn't actually have its own Table (too small, insignificant) — it falls 'in the approaches' of Rye Bay and Hastings, but even so, it still doesn't demand much basic common sense to puzzle the tides out. I didn't tarry to make this calculation, though, just grabbed my keys and my wallet (no. Not the keys — just the wallet) and blithely set off. It was a silly scheme. It would be fair to say that I sincerely regret it, now. I do. I really do. I regret the leaving, but gracious me! The return! When I finally dragged my way back home (no bus fare! That endless trudge from Hastings over hard road and soggy field!)... On my eventual...

I see it clear as day in my mind's eye: that lone dustbin perched — somewhat improbably — atop the Look Out (visible from quite some distance off). A warning shot across my bows. An omen. But I just gazed at it, quite innocently, idly pondering the logistics of it all. How on earth did that...? I mean it's a difficult enough scramble up there without...

I was just way too frazzled to register that this was *my* bin, that this was *my* issue...

Perhaps I was actually heading for the New Beach Club (that previous afternoon but one) although the NBC is actually in the opposite direction to Hastings, so possibly not. Or, better still, to The Smuggler (which is *en route*), for a stiff drink or three. I don't precisely recall. Although I was dangerously short of cash. Yes. Only had enough for a Schweppes bitter lemon or a Coke. Perhaps I was just...

What was I doing?
Letting off steam?
Getting some much-needed air?
Thinking things through on the hoof?
Walking it out?

All of the above?

I don't really know why I left (it's honestly just a blur now – a pointless irrel-evance), but then to return to... I mean to come back to the cottage (my *base*, my *home*, my... my *lair*), stagger into the bedroom – exhausted, depleted – and find... *Urgh!*

The bin was definitely a warning. Then the porch light wouldn't work. The bulb was missing. Then...

*Urgh. Urgh. Urgh!*

It now occurs to me that perhaps I hadn't taken the news of Kimberly's passing quite so well as I'd initially thought. How I loathe that word: 'passing'! It smacks of the clairvoyant: the velvet curtain, the spotlight, the odour of a cheap cigar. It's a verb which tiptoes gingerly around the ineffable absolutes of mortality; the stiffness, the coldness, the imminent putrescence. The ineluctable *gone*-ness.

'Passing'. It's an end without an end – an end without a beginning, even. A cowardly avoidance.

But how else to... to get through all those unbearable sentences – those endless, stewing thoughts – each one punctuated by the thudding, hammer-blow of 'dead'? That savage, nail-in-the-coffin word. I used it – I *had* used it – countless times in the first short while after hearing the news (that garbled phone message), but its regular use – all that relentless thud-thud-thudding – had begun to bump and bruise my *very core*. The body was inside the coffin! Bang, bang, bang! The lid was sealed! Bang, bang, bang! But still the word kept on providing new nails, and of course they needed to be applied (demanded it) – to be neatly and dispassionately embedded. But where? The wall? the door? My heart? My head? My soul? *No!* No, I had to get rid of that word. I had to eliminate it. It had suddenly become too real, too meaningful. How even to approach it now without... without feeling the urge to emit a terrible, wolf-like howl? Without jabbering? Without flailing around? Falling to my knees and tearing at my clothes? Without an all-out collapse, in other words? Surely it's better to just... just use something else, something less definitive, something that evades... that compresses... that *curtails* the connected emotion. A band-aid word. Yes. A slightly vague, pointless, polite, peripheral word. To cleverly create a separate universe in language and then quietly retreat into it, to hide, like a cringing ninny, from... from... From Kimberly's passing?

Yes.

Kimberly has passed... Oh, look! There she goes! Hear the whistle? Kimberly! She's a heavy-goods train thundering through the station of life (no timetabled stop) and then into the glorious bleakness – the billowing clouds of dry ice – beyond. Only the truly adventurous – the demented hobo, the illegal, the felon – would consider running after her and hitching a ride. Those trains are heavily guarded, I've heard. No. Better just wait a little longer on the welcoming, well-lit platform and flick through the local paper (great article about piles. Wonderful small ads. Nothing really amounting to 'news,' as such) then head over to the kiosk for a hot cup of coffee (Avoid the tea. The tea's dreadful, like warm iron filings. It's been stewing for days inside a giant rusty urn).

Just stand back (always respectful, mind) and let that old, heavy-goods train rumble on through...

Rumble.

*Rrrrrumble?*

Gracious me! A sudden outbreak of goose-bumps on my forearm. How odd!

Uh...

No.

No. Let's not talk of death, eh? Death sticks between the teeth like a pesky piece of sweet corn husk. Sweetcorn's way too ambitious a vegetable for a man in my state. I need mashed potato softened with milk. Or mushy peas. Or a lightly seasoned dollop of glowing swede, shining with butter. Or porridge. I need porridge! I need custard! A soft-boiled egg!

I'm too delicate!

Coddle me!

Uh...

No.

It wasn't a great scheme, in other words. I wasn't genned up on the Tide Times. I just headed out – flew out.

Perhaps I was more upset than I thought. Everything felt very sharp – the light, the sound of the gulls, the *waves* – the damn Channel so unapologetic, so vital, so unbearably bloody *there* – the texture of the pebbles on the beach, the individual grains of sand... Everything sharp. Everything cruel. And then... What happened? I'm struggling to... uh...

Ten paces after I saw Ms Hahn and her ridiculous dog – that awful, fat dog; a barely-perambulating canine offence, a cruel joke – I suddenly stopped short and thought, 'God. Did I actually just *say* that? Did I actually just speak those words from here... up here... from this mouth?' The exchange – *was* there an exchange, though? – fell across the beach in front of me like a shadow in bright sun. I moved, it moved. Good Heavens! Did I actually just...? No. Surely not! So I promptly strode on. Had to get through it. Simple as that. Fight or flight. Fight *and* flight. Pure instinct. Couldn't think. Didn't want to. Continued walking.

It's possible the plan hadn't even been fully hatched at that stage – the epic hike. It was barely in incubation. I was just... still can't quite remember what I... I think it was just... just getting away from that word. The relentless hammer-blow of that word.

'Good afternoon, Ms Hahn! The renovations? Uh... not now, dear. I'm... uh...

F

My wife just died. We weren't really married... well we were, but in title alone. We lived on separate continents. But I still reserve the right to be *intensely* pissed off – alternately numbed, bewildered, *shattered*, even – by the news. Alright, Ms Hahn? Okay with that, are we? Is that *acceptable* to you Ms Hahn? It is? It *is*? Good! Great! Toodle–oo!'

I just... I just... I wanted to blurt it out! Yes! I wanted to castigate, to blame – worse still, to *share*. I felt this sudden, overwhelming urge to unload! To unburden, to spill out my guts to that awful Ms Hahn with her... her frayed collar, her fat dog, her man's trousers and her Soviet–style nose. But why *her*? Why then? Why there? *Eh*?!

Happenstance. Pure happenstance! A fluke. She could've been anyone! That's why. And worse still, I'm sure I even found myself thinking: eyes on the prize, Franklin! This could actually prove useful – playing the sympathy card! I did! I swear! But then I suddenly realised (hammer blow – *bang!*) that without Kimberly there *was* no meaning – no book (and no Advance! *Bang, bang!* Double whammy!). And I also realised that I couldn't play the card if I didn't accept the feeling. And I didn't accept it. No! I just didn't. So I stopped myself. I tried to find a suitable cover for my confusion. My mind was racing (but there was no race, no track, just miles and miles of empty *air*) and I found myself blurting out... Uh... What? Did I say that the dog was fat? Yes. Yes. I think I did, actually. But then the dog *is* fat. Big deal! I merely stated a known fact! No harm done there, then.

And so I calmly walked on. And a while later it started to rain. And I can remember the pebbles and the rocks all shiny in the wet. And my shoes – dress shoes – splattered with mud. And I remember how high the cliffs were. So high. So improbably high... *Woo! Woo-hoo!* (I'm spinning around, gazing upwards, woo-hooing, like a jack–ass)... Oh look – *there*... See that black bird, just circling above? Is it a raven? A chough? Do they even *have* choughs in this part of the British Isles? Or ravens for that matter? Uh... No. Possibly not. What's that...? (Stops spinning, staggers slightly). What's that extraordinary... uh...?

And then... And then – *Wham! Bam! Alakazam!* – forty–eight hours had passed me by, in what felt like the merest of breaths, and I was waking up in the cells with the mother of all hangovers, a tin bucket by the bed, splayed across a creepy, squeaky, rubber–coated mattress, no bed linen, no blanket, not so much as a *pillow* – a humble pillow – to rest my pounding head upon.

Oh. And there was a baby rabbit tucked away snugly inside my vest. My suit was still wet. The pockets were full of leaves. White Ash? Eucalyptus? After approximately five minutes a young constable brought me some sweet tea and said that they were releasing me without charge but I needed to provide them with some details of my identity. I had no idea at this stage that I was missing an entire day. A day had been stolen! But by whom?! My wallet (a matter of secondary importance – it was empty, remember?) was also gone. Apparently I'd been apprehended by a passing member of the local foot patrol – in riotous mood (me, not the copper) – drinking on the beach the previous morning with a couple of reprobate old fisher-folk. I'd tried to break into a church: Saint Thomas of Canterbury and the English Martyrs (in St Leonards) which contains exquisite painted murals (stencils, but still lovely) by Nathaniel Westlake, no less. Amazing. Yes – *yes!* I *had* broken in (I have no memory of this) and I'd confessed a pile of hysterical mumbo-jumbo, in Spanish, to the priest, then kneeled and prayed with him (we'd conversed freely – he was born and raised in Alicante) then jumped up and ran off. I'd tried to make a sled out of a bakery pallet and had careered down the Old London Road on it (I was relatively successful, in other words), ending up in a large bush of Pampas Grass (slightly cut lip – evidence of white fluff in hair). I had stolen and eaten half a loaf. I was wearing lipstick (yes!). Orange lipstick. In giant circles around my eyes. Three cigarettes had been stubbed out on the top of my hand. My right hand. And the rabbit? A dwarf breed. Quite rare. Of indeterminate age, it transpires. Nobody knew where it had come from, only that I'd been finding great solace in it. The officer had kindly fed it a carrot.

It was a white rabbit with pink eyes. I walked all the way home with it held in a makeshift sling fashioned out of my jacket. Even now I find it incredible to think that I would have walked all that way with it. I am no fan of small mammals. I have given it a temporary berth in the bath. In the bath the enamel turns its white fur a yellower hue. Strange how the act of comparison can suddenly transform one clearly defined object into something else altogether. Life has a nasty habit of doing that.

I noticed that there was a tiny hole in the bathroom window. Later on I found an even tinier stone in the toilet bowl.

But that was not all I found. Oh no. The bin, the missing bulb, the hole in the window (all serious, in their own way, admittedly) were as nothing by comparison (that rabbit in the bath phenomenon, remember?) with the thing I found in my bedroom. I say 'thing', but it was more than a mere 'thing', it was a performance, a staging, an extravaganza. It was a complete one-act drama. I hate to oversell it, but... come with me. Enter the room. Push open the door and then grimacingly recoil. There is a smell... Not even a smell, a stink, a vile, ungodly odour. Something so foul, so rank, that mere words – simple, uncomplicated *language* – cannot do justice to its offensiveness. A slap in the face. A *physical* reaction. A *gut* reaction. A violent recoil. An existential shudder. A withering of the soul. A shrinking. A boring at the nostril. A tearing at the throat.

But where? From whence doth this rancid odour hail, pray tell? (I've fallen into Olde English in a pathetic attempt to try and encompass how *primordial* this smell is, how primitive, how base, how... how *medieval* – and how fearful I am, how confused, how repulsed; but still pretending, nevertheless, to be bold, pretending to be jocular;

F

call to mind, if you must, a cheery fifteenth-century soldier – a Man of Fortune – or, better still, a palsied whore or cocky jester.) I search the room, a shirt over my face. My forehead is instantly dripping with sweat. My hand is a claw. I am a zombie. My body is panicking. It's instinctive. The smell is so... so *engulfing*.

Eventually I settle on my suitcase, my empty suitcase (old leather, a gift from my maternal grandfather when I went up to Cambridge). It lies under the bed. I drag it out by its handle. I am so full of dread. Hands shaking. Palms wet. I steady myself. My heart is pounding. One, two, three – Come on, Franklin! Grow some balls, man! – I throw open the lid.

*NNNAAAAARRRRRGGHHHH!*

So much worse – so, so much worse – than I could possibly have anticipated! Several hundred huge, buzzing bluebottles swarm out of the case and into my face. It is as though the devil himself (I'm an atheist, but bear with me) has been compressed in that small space. And now he is free. And he is angry. The *sound!* The intensity of that roar! The violence of those wings! The sense of un... un... unexpurgated *filth!* And remaining? In the case? The putrefying corpse of a dead shark. A dead *sand* shark, no less.

Urgh!

*Urgh!*

I vomited – instantly, spontaneously – onto my own, damp lap.

The sheer indignity!

Words cannot do justice. No. *No.* Sometimes, even justice – even *justice* – cannot do justice.

This is an excerpt from *IN THE APPROACHES*, forthcoming from 4th Estate in June 2014.

# INTERVIEW

WITH

# LYDIA DAVIS

AT ONLY FORTY-EIGHT WORDS IN LENGTH, the title story of Lydia Davis's latest collection, CAN'T AND WON'T (2014), is characteristically concise. The narrator reflects on having been 'denied a writing prize', because 'I would not write in full the words cannot and will not, but instead contracted them to can't and won't.' As in many of Davis's stories, this anecdote seems disconcertingly personal. Nonetheless, life and art never completely align. Davis herself has won numerous awards (including, most recently, the Man Booker International Prize) for her sparse and 'contracted' pieces of prose. The question of just how to categorise these texts – are they simply 'stories', or do they come closer to essays, pensées, philosophical investigations? – has been repeatedly raised, and yet is irresoluble. Perhaps because of her work's elusiveness (and partly, too, because of her intimidating intellect) I approached the interview with apprehension.

Often for critics it doesn't suffice to say that a novel or a story simply 'is'. Instead, it must also be made to *mean* something – something safely susceptible to critical explanation, such as might validate criticism's continued existence. In this sense, I came to our conversation with a critic's keenness to extrapolate; to contextualise; even to theorise. But I came away with something quite different. Davis is one of the most open and generous authors I've ever interviewed. At the same time, to discuss her writing is to feel oneself slipping along its surface, glimpsing without grasping depths that are largely unseen and unspoken. For all the brevity of her very short stories – and perhaps not despite, but precisely because of their apparent banality – they evoke a mystery that cannot be captured by critical commentary. Indeed, Davis's mind seems to inhabit the same element as her fiction; her answers to my questions are straightforward and unassuming, yet suggestive of numerous nuances and implications. If there are lessons to be learned from her work, then, this would be one of them: although we are quick to complicate things, what seems simple is complex enough.

———

Q. THE WHITE REVIEW — You've often ob-served that you grew up in a household not only where there were a lot of books, but also where people were particularly conscious of language, or tended to foreground language, at more of a formal or grammatical level. Could we start with a sketch of the way this shaped your sensibility, as a reader and writer?

A. LYDIA DAVIS — My father was a fic-tion writer early on in his career, and later a critic and English professor. My mother was a writer of short stories, book reviews, and eventually a memoir. So, for as long as I can remember, they were busy with writing proj-ects, and would then read each other's work and discuss it. There was always that hour or so of dramatic tension in the house while one was reading the other's work and I had to be very quiet.

Yes, there were books everywhere, and always a dictionary open on a book stand in the living room. My father would often go over to the dictionary to look up a word, usu-ally to find out its derivation. Then he would announce to us what it was. Once, when he looked up a word and read the supporting quote, he discovered that the authority being quoted was himself.

This does not mean that it was a family of deadly seriousness. My parents were indeed serious about how language was used, about exact expression, but they also had a sense of humour and fun. They liked to play games in the evening, and I don't mean psychological games, but card games, roulette... They liked to watch certain TV shows, like PERRY MASON. They gossiped about neighbours and other faculty, and their friends. My father liked to amuse us, and to make bad puns. So, they were serious without being pedantic.

But they did correct me if I did not express myself well. My grammar would not have been the problem, since it was quite good, but they might perhaps point out a careless repetition. I think the fact that writing and language were so constantly discussed, and that our spoken language was always heard and appraised, and that my own writing for school would be read with interest by them was like an ongoing intensive tutorial in writing – ongoing for years, of course, even decades. I don't remember finding this oppressive, since after all, the conversations were lively and interesting, and we had enjoyable times. But it did make me a bit self-conscious when speaking. And the result was that I can't help paying attention to language all the time – spoken, written by me, written by others. And I don't find this oppressive, either, since this language is saying something, after all. I find it constantly engrossing.

Q. THE WHITE REVIEW —— One of the most striking things about your writing is its apparent 'ordinariness' of idiom. Of course, the linguistic world of your stories isn't exactly the same as that of everyday speech – the sentences seem shaped by an unusual degree of 'attention' or 'self-consciousness', to use your terms. Yet you're able to achieve, while remaining within a relatively conventional register, the kinds of effects (effects of estrangement and

defamiliarisation, say) that other writers might only manage in a much more stylised, more overtly 'literary' mode. Could I ask about the importance of the ordinary in your stories?

A. LYDIA DAVIS —— One of the difficult aspects of certain questions about my writing is that I'm asked to articulate a process that is, for me, instinctual, relatively unthinking, at least in its first stages. I don't ask myself, ahead of time – before beginning to write a story – what effect I want, or how I will achieve that effect. Rather, my attention is not on myself or my writing, but on the thing that has inspired me. A situation or idea inspires or excites me; I then try to capture that situation or idea as exactly as possible, with no more words than necessary, but no fewer either. The language will be simple, sometimes to an extreme; and sometimes repetitious, but not for the sake of repetition itself, only in order to be absolutely clear. The kind of language I use in writing a story is natural to me, probably very like the language I use in speaking – though the syntax is not the syntax of my speech. I can say that one thing I admired about Beckett, early on, when I was actively learning from him, was that he used very ordinary or plain language to create conceptually or philosophically or even mathematically complex situations. A multi-syllabic and abstract word like 'defamiliarisation' would not be a natural part of my working vocabulary, for instance, but I might achieve that effect, as you say – the effect of defamiliarisation – using very ordinary or plain language.

I suppose I see abstract or complex language as somewhat distancing, though not everyone would see it that way. I see plainer or more ordinary language as drawing me closer to the thing I am writing about, involving me with it more intimately. I find plain language more emotional, more moving. And yet, as I said about Beckett's situations, plain language can be used to describe complex situations. There is also a physical beauty to plain language that I don't find in highly abstract language.

Actually, in looking for an example of plain language that I wanted to quote for you, I just came across another note, which was of something Churchill is reputed to have said. (I know that some of his purported remarks are not really his.) This is what he is said to have said: 'Broadly speaking,' – and I would leave off those first two words – 'the short words are best, and the old words are best of all.' I like that idea, and I like the simplicity of the way he expressed it. But then, among the short and old words, I might throw in a slightly longer word, like 'balefully', and enjoy its effect by contrast with the monosyllables.

Now here is the quote I was looking for. It goes beyond being ordinary – or rather it is ordinary to such a different time and place, being an example of Lowland Scots of the nineteenth century, that it is in fact exotic to us: 'He could nether hud nor binn.' I can almost feel those words in my mouth, though I can't at the moment recall exactly what they mean.

Q. THE WHITE REVIEW —— Reading your work, I'm sometimes reminded of Wittgenstein's line about Tolstoy: 'His philosophy is most true when it's latent in the story.' Perhaps your stories support the idea that fiction is most 'philosophical' in a latent sense – just as philosophy could be said to inhere implicitly in daily life. For instance, your chapbook THE COWS reflects some of what you've said above. The cows that graze near your house are 'often like a math problem', you write, and 'just because they are so still, their attitude seems philosophical'. Is there anything you want to say about this particular piece of writing?

What was it about the situation – three cows in a field – that inspired you?

A. LYDIA DAVIS —— It's a little odd to talk about this, as though in the abstract, and as though it's well in the past, because I can still look out the window – I did earlier today – and see three black cows out there in the field across the road, though in fact only one of them is one of the original three cows that I wrote about. (And one of them is not a cow, but a young bull that still nurses from its mother occasionally, though it's about eight months old now and quite large – which tells me something about what a young bull needs, or at least wants.)

The piece developed in a very natural, organic way. When we moved here, about seven years ago – farther into the country than we had been before – the field across the road was empty, though there was an old red barn next to it. I thought how nice it would be if there were some kind of animal in the field. And just a few months later, quite by chance, the neighbours brought in three heifers. I liked to look out the window at them and began to write down things I saw that interested me. I didn't think of making anything out of these observations. But as time went by, the observations accumulated, and I thought I should gather them together, which is what I did. I then arranged them in a way that made sense to me – not chronologically as they had occurred, but in a sequence that moved from morning to night and from fall through winter to spring, when two calves were born.

I thought I was simply writing down what I observed and thought about the cows, but after a while, when I read over what I had written, I saw that the piece was also about looking – about patterns, perspective, distortion, shape, illusion – though of course it was also about the cows themselves, and how they would, for instance, just stand still for a long time in the snow-covered winter pasture, without doing anything at all – a strange thing for a busy human being to comprehend.

Q. THE WHITE REVIEW —— A somewhat similar process – an accumulation of observations, and an 'arrangement' of those observations according to a logic that doesn't quite equate to a typical 'narrative' – seems to structure your only novel, THE END OF THE STORY. Would you like to talk a bit about the composition of this book? I think I can see certain continuities of approach between THE END OF THE STORY and your short stories, but presumably the long form posed its own particular challenges?

A. LYDIA DAVIS —— Yes, the novel does work by accumulation, to some extent. I could say that the premise is that this narrator has certain things she wants to say about the love affair, and the man himself, either longer or shorter things, and she is anxious to express them as clearly and completely as possible, and find some arrangement for them that makes sense. So she not only tells the story of the love affair but also talks about the difficulty of writing it down, finding an order for its different parts. This premise – that it is a sort of monologue, rather than a more traditionally constructed novel with scenes and extensive dialogue – explains the form of it. When I was beginning it, I looked for good models, and one was the novels of Thomas Bernhard, another was Elizabeth Hardwick's SLEEPLESS NIGHTS, and another was Marguerite Duras's THE LOVER and also WAR.

In fact, it started as two different novels that were then merged. One was a more artificial narration of the love affair, which I was not so fond of. So I began, at the same time, something that felt rather subversive – the 'secret' novel – which I called Novel II and which confided how difficult it was to write

Novel I, and talked in some detail about the difficulty. That one I enjoyed very much. So then I decided to put the two together into one. Novel I in the process became much less artificial, and the two narratives, I thought, offset each other well.

One of the difficulties for me in writing the novel was that I was so used to the short form, which was my more natural form, that I found organising the novel quite a challenge. One can 'see' or hold in one's head all of a short piece at once, one has a sense of its proportions and pacing. A longer work is hard to grasp in its totality. I eventually had to make a diagram, with a red line for one time period of the story, the past, and a blue line for the present and the narration of constructing the novel. I wanted the red and blue lines to be roughly equal in length overall, and I didn't want either line to continue too long without the other reappearing. That diagram was helpful.

Another challenge the long form had that the short form did not was that I had to begin again each day and find the same energy or forward impetus. With a short piece, the whole thing is often written in an hour or two, in its first draft anyway. The novel goes on for weeks and weeks, or months and months. You have to find a way of controlling it and yet still being spontaneous and allowing for the unexpected.

Q. THE WHITE REVIEW —— In this respect, the long and short forms also entail different reading experiences. For a start there's a temporal difference, in terms of how long it takes to read these two types of text. But there's also another kind of contrast, connected, perhaps, to certain generic preconceptions: short stories feel more ephemeral, and are often unfairly regarded as a writer's 'minor' works, if she or he has also written novels. There's a sense in which stories seem closer to sketches, or fragments, whereas the idea of 'the book' evokes completion and accomplishment. Actually, I was struck by this when reading your COLLECTED STORIES. I read it cover to cover, rather than dipping in and out, and its cumulative effect altered its component parts: somehow the stories looked different in the light of an oeuvre. Maybe that's just me – but at any rate, there's something interesting about the way collections of stories take shape, and the way their shape affects their contents. Is there a logic to the way you put these books together?

A. LYDIA DAVIS —— Yes, I've heard, or read, that the cumulative effect of reading at length in the COLLECTED STORIES is quite different from reading one or two at a time, dipping into it, as you say. I will never know that effect, I suppose, because I simply can't imagine reading it from beginning to end myself. It's true that I've now read my forthcoming collection of stories from beginning to end several times over, in order to check the galleys. But because I'm reading slowly and looking for typos, that is a different experience again.

It's true that people make a false equation between size and quality, often, so that bigger seems better or more important. (There is that curious statistic, or finding, that more tall men, proportionally, than small men occupy positions at the heads of companies.) And the sheer effort of producing a novel is something I admire even when the novel isn't very good. Can a gem of a story have the same power as a novel? There is the effect of the time spent living with – experiencing – the novel. That can't be matched. Think of Joyce's 'Araby' and 'The Dead'. They are both powerful. But is 'The Dead' more powerful in part because it takes more time unfolding and developing? I seem to be defending length, but I'm really just thinking aloud.

But to return to your question about how my books were put together. In one sense, each individual collection was put together in a fairly pragmatic way. I'll explain. First, though, to answer a question you didn't ask but that I am sometimes asked: I've never planned out a collection of stories before they were written; I've never said to myself, 'Oh, I'd like to write a collection of stories with this or that theme.' No, each individual story has come into being on its own, as an individual. I write a particular story with no thought of a book, until, after a time, I see that I have quite a number of finished stories. Enough for a book? I wonder, and start counting. Sometimes I'll see that there are too many stories about this or that subject, and I'll leave some out – reserve them for the next book. Similarly, I'll decide that a few more are needed, quite different. In that case, I never write a story deliberately to add to a collection. I either wait until a few more stories are written, or – and this has happened in all the collections, I think – I look back to quite early work, work in small press books that are out of print, and take a few stories that I think deserve to live on, and add them to the collection I am putting together.

Then I put the stories in some sort of order, which is quite a task when there are over fifty stories, or, as in the forthcoming book, over a hundred. Often the logic is: put some strong, punchy ones at the beginning and the same at the end; put the longer, more sober or thoughtful stories somewhere after the middle, where there is room for something meditative; try not to bunch too many of the same sort together; but sometimes it's nice to put a couple together that seem to be speaking to each other. Watch out that the end of one doesn't echo too much the beginning of the next. And so on – many little decisions and a lot of moving the stories around. Sometimes the order never seems quite right – but then, as we know, many people don't read the collection from beginning to end anyway.

Q. THE WHITE REVIEW — Alongside Flaubert and Proust, you've also translated multiple texts by Maurice Blanchot – his récits as well as his literary/philosophical essays. Looking back, I was fairly familiar with your work on Blanchot before I came to your fiction – so that, rightly or wrongly, the former coloured my reading of the latter. It might be too crude to frame this question in terms of 'influence', but I assume that Blanchot has been a source of deep fascination for you. If so, could you describe that fascination?

A. LYDIA DAVIS — I began translating Blanchot – his L'ARRÊT DE MORT – when I was at a standstill with some writing of my own and a friend suggested taking a break to tackle a different sort of project. This was sometime in the early Seventies. I did feel quite an affinity with Blanchot as I worked on his prose over the years from then on. I translated six books altogether, though one was quite short – LA FOLIE DU JOUR. What appealed to me, most likely, was his deep exploration of a single emotion, or thought, or interaction; his patience; the many levels at which his 'plots' unfold – so that not only the actual people in the scene interact, but also their thoughts and emotions; even the absence of a person becomes a character, or the lack of an emotion, or the possibility of a thought, or the illusion of a perception, etc. Abstractions, in other words, become living entities with strong effects. All this is narrated in a plain, straightforward way that is immensely respectful of language, thinking, human nature. I'm talking about the récits, of course.

As for the essays, they are also multilayered and complex. I translated only one book of essays, which was a collection taken from different volumes in French. I found them difficult to translate, at times. There were sentences whose meaning I simply could not grasp. I wonder if I would have any better luck if I returned to those sentences today. Maybe my at times intense struggle to comprehend one of his sentences was good practice for my following Proust's long and elaborately constructed prose.

One curious feature of reading Blanchot's essays, for me, anyway, was that in the case of certain of them, although I could follow his argument as I read it, I found it hard, or impossible, to summarise: I could not step back and give you the gist of what he had said – I did not come away with anything like 'the gist'. I imagined that this might be a result of my own mental failing, until I talked to others who had the same reaction. Of course this is not true of all the essays.

During these years, I had the pleasure of corresponding with Blanchot. He was unfailingly kind, gracious, and modest.

Q. THE WHITE REVIEW — Your new collection, CAN'T AND WON'T, contains a number of 'dream pieces', which are often only a paragraph long. I found these particularly captivating. Personally, I've never quite understood the well-known saying, 'Nothing is so boring as listening to someone else describe a dream.' Boredom can become an interesting thing in itself. But besides that, there's also a long tradition of literary dream diaries, which I find far from boring – from Michel Leiris to Georges Perec to Graham Greene. Were you thinking about such precursors while you worked on these pieces? What inspired you to write in this mode, and how did you go about it?

A. LYDIA DAVIS — A dream certainly is a

curious psychic and physical phenomenon. I haven't read much about what goes on physiologically when one dreams, but I did read that a certain part of the brain shuts down – the part that would deny the reality of what is happening in the dream. So, as you dream the wildest things, you believe them. This means that the dream is intensely real, and often emotional. When you wake, you feel that you have been through that real experience, even though you distance yourself a little from it, since you know it was a dream.

I think that is why it is sometimes difficult to listen to other people's dreams – to them the dream is still half real, and emotional, while to you it is not, and you look on from the outside as they re-experience something in which you had no part, and which was, moreover – you sensibly say – not real.

For a long time, I did not have a great deal of interest in dreams or the dreaming life, but I did have on my shelf the book you are thinking of, by Michel Leiris, which in the English translation by Richard Sieburth is called NIGHTS AS DAY, DAYS AS NIGHT. I like what Leiris does in the volume, which is to intermingle accounts of dreams he had while sleeping with accounts of events in his waking life that were like dreams. Then, one day, I had an experience, out driving in the car, which was so dream-like that I was taken right to Leiris's book. My husband was at the wheel and I was navigating. We were going from one town to another, about half an hour from where we live. For a change, I suggested a route that ran parallel to the more heavily travelled route. The road we took was good for a while, but then gradually disappeared: it became rougher and narrower, and eventually ended up no more than a rocky track in some dense woods. This, even though on the paper map I held in my hands, it appeared to lead right into the town we were headed for. We had to turn around, with difficulty, and go back.

What I became interested in, I think, was that thin line between the dream-like features of certain of our waking experiences and the odd strain of reality that may run through even our stranger night dreams. I thought it would be interesting to narrate both in the same way, so as to blur the line between them – to learn how to write an account whose very style would cause it to sound like a dream, whether it was or not.

So, for quite a while, maybe a couple of years, I was on the alert, looking for possible dream material. I wrote down my own actual night dreams, selecting only the parts of them that formed a coherent little narrative, however short or fragmentary. I watched out for waking experiences that could be narrated, selectively, to sound like dreams. And I went farther afield and used friends' experiences and friends' dreams to create more of these narratives. The dream story about pushing a piano over a cliff, for instance, came from material in an old letter of my sister's, and what she wrote was not a dream and not fictional. Part of the challenge was stylistic – to get back to your initial point about the danger of boredom: in the shadow of that danger, of our association of dream narratives with boredom, how to shape each account in a tight and compelling way, and how to narrate the dream in language that had the tension of reality.

♀ THE WHITE REVIEW — In your story 'Not Interested' the narrator claims to 'prefer books that contain something real, or something the author at least believed to be real,' as opposed to books based purely upon 'the imagination'. Similarly, your stories often seem to revolve either around something apparently 'real' (for instance, a found text like the one in 'Example of Continuing Past Tense in a Hotel Room') or something 'believed' to be so (such as a dream, or maybe a memory). This might be an almost impossibly broad question to close with, but to what degree does a pursuit of 'reality' – or what you've called the 'tension of reality' – drive what you're trying to do, as a writer?

A. LYDIA DAVIS —— Well, your last question makes me think hard about this – invention versus the manipulation of 'reality'. Why has my evolution taken this particular direction? It is true that over the years I have become less interested in the wholly invented fictional story, and more interested in the story that is composed using real events or situations or scenes – or fragments thereof – with minor fictional elements. It is true that my great pleasure, now, is coming upon the gems that occur all the time in real life events and real dialogue, noting them down, and either doing something with them or never using them, in the end. Such pleasures as the redundancy in this announcement: 'A reminder that today the community will be gathering this afternoon to come together as a community.' Or the weather reporter's choice of verb, when, this morning, she says there is a lot of ice 'situated' on the tree limbs. Or a friend tells me a story about a man who separates from his wife Pearline, needs a housekeeper, and finds one named Pearl (in a story, I might reverse the names). Or something even simpler: in a local obituary for 'Laura', the observation that 'she enjoyed walking around the village'.

So, I collect these – sometimes they are even plainer. For instance, I was reading about the physiology of dreaming, in part because of your earlier question, and I found this nice sentence, which describes my own experience of dreaming: 'It is impossible to scream.' Or, after a dinner with friends during which we have been talking about our eating habits, I articulate one friend's position with the following sentence, which I like for its extreme, scientific precision: his diet is entirely vegan, with the exception of bivalves, which, he says, though possessing nociceptors, do not really experience pain. A few more, one from a newsletter: 'It's cold outside, but your library is warm.' Another from an advertising flyer: 'Together we will find the perfect flooring.' Another from an email: 'Alas, I'm in Denver.' These are small tidbits, but they please me, and I see that they please me because of the way they use language. Even if I don't import them directly into a piece of writing, I may be learning something, assimilating something, from their tone and even from the implied character or personality of the speaker, something that may find its way into the narrative tone of a story.

A large part of writing a story, after all, has to do with structure, proportion, the ordering of events and facts, and of course the choice and handling of the language itself – in description, striving for precision and minutely observed detail (à la Flaubert), and in dialogue, the economical expressiveness of one's characters. The material can be invented, or it can be real. In a way, it doesn't matter. Invented material can be wonderful. As for a story using 'real' material, what makes it read as fiction is the tone, the stylised nature of the writing, the selection and shaping of the material, and of course those (optional) fictional elements that may be needed for the structure or drama of it. Out of a hundred people reading this sort of story, though, only three might know that it has many 'real' elements; to the other ninety-seven, it could just as well be wholly invented.

So, these days, I'm simply more interested in the manipulation of material taken from everyday life – which of course can include texts. It feels like a great, rich mine. Every time I tap it, I find something wonderful, whether I'm reading the schedule of events at the local library ('Dental Care with Puppets'), or the diary of an ancestor (a sea captain who comes out on deck in his nightshirt to look at the full moon), or the report of a complaint – with its touch of the biblical – concerning a Manhattan apartment building ('The above address has an improper drainage as a result there is standing water and it has caused the plants to sprout from the ground.').

When I am working with reality, the material is all there, or almost all, and my challenge is to put it into a form that suits it, and then to arrange it and word it effectively, making little adjustments or fictional additions to the 'truth' as necessary. Invention is not obligatory. Maybe it is my long practice of translation that has biased me toward the pleasure of working with found material – an important difference, however, being that I have a great deal more freedom with a story of my own.

DAVID WINTERS, FEBRUARY 2014

# POSITIONS

BY

# ISABELLE WENZEL

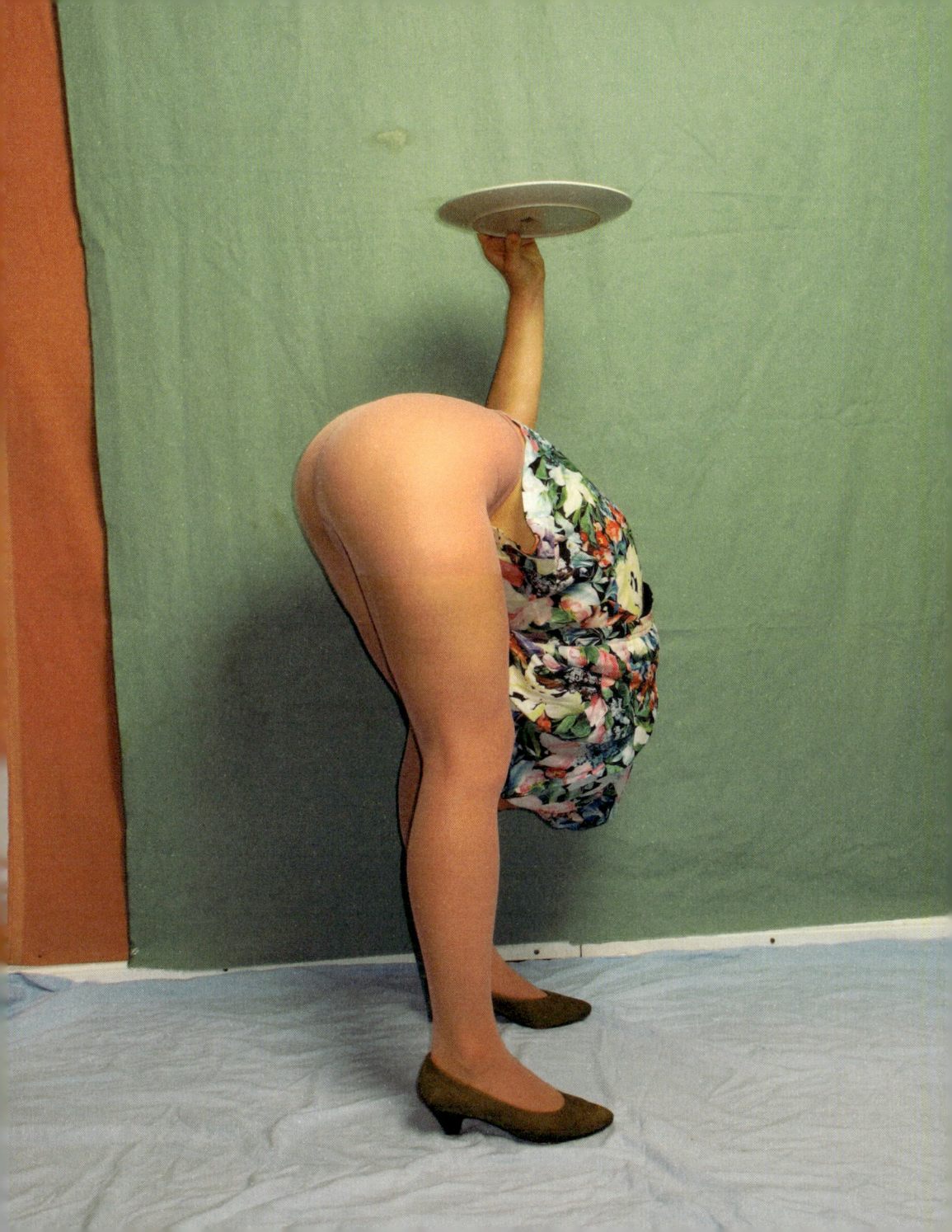

# URGENCY
# AND PATIENCE

## BY

# JEAN-PHILIPPE
# TOUSSAINT

(*tr.* EDWARD GAUVIN)

WHEN I'M WRITING A BOOK, I want to be airborne, breezy of mind and blithe of hand. My arse. I'm actually very organised. I train myself, prepare myself, prime myself. There's something monastic in my attitude – something Spartan, something of the lonely sailor. Everything matters: physical condition, diet, reading. When I'm writing, I sleep early and abstain from alcohol. During the day, I go for a walk, a bike ride, a swim – swimming has never failed to go well with study, quite the opposite. Until RETICENCE, whenever I embarked on a book, I would work all day, every day, without coming up for air, without taking a break, up to a year at a time. I thought of writing as heavy equipment in place for the long run, something steady, weighty, hindersome; something that refused to give, that stumbled, that advanced effortfully, inch by inch – a plough.

The painful experience of writing RETICENCE, a book I was not managing to write, which I almost gave up on multiple times – I was mired, couldn't muddle through, but I gritted my teeth, kept digging, clung on, calling upon the figure of Kafka and the most dolorous ideals of writing – this painful experience led to my decision never to write this way again. I no longer wanted to suffer like this; I had to change my approach. From then on, I have only worked when borne by some momentum, in writing sessions of limited duration, for a fortnight to three months tops, punctuated by long periods of doing something else – not writing, living – which can be useful as well.

> I've always had remarkable success with this sort of mental labour, it's true, letting the book come to gradually settle in and inhabit me by simply following the thread of my thoughts, doing nothing that might interrupt the flow, and so unchaining a multitude of impressions and reveries, a host of structures and ideas, often incomplete, scattered, unformed, some still gestating, some already fully developed, a wealth of intuitions and insights, of pains and emotions, which I then had only to put into their definitive form... And... I reflected that, if your goal is to write, not writing is surely at least as important as writing. (TELEVISION, trans. Jordan Stump, 51-52; Dalkey Archive Press, 2004)

Until RETICENCE, it would take me about a year to write a book, but now the same number of actual working hours is spread out over three. I don't work at home, in Brussels, but in Corsica, or Ostend. In Ostend, I rent an apartment, a neutral space. I like the hermit crab aspect of a guest who moves into a shell not his own. The places where I work are always temporary, put to other uses in my absence. Sometimes other people live in the Ostend apartment, and the large room where I write in Corsica serves another purpose when I'm not there. I show up, claim these places for myself, set up shop: computer, printer, research. When I go, I take everything with me, and leave no traces of my passage.

I like the idea that a book can be defined as a 'dream in stone' (the words are Baudelaire's). 'Dream' because of the freedom it demands — daring, risk, fantasy, the unknown; 'stone' because of the consistency — firm, solid, mineral — obtained through sheer, unrelenting work on language, words, and grammar. When you've got your nose too deep in a manuscript, your eyes in the gears and grease of sentences, sometimes you lose sight of the line of a book. I like picturing a book as a line. I like the abstraction of it, where literature meets music, where the book's line rises, falls, and billows according to the dictates of rhythm. Sometimes a contradiction arises between my desire to write lasting sentences, almost aphorisms, and the need for such sentences not to stop reading short, not even to slow it down. These sentences must be swept up in the course of the novel without disturbing its flow, must burrow into the text, almost camouflaged, so that they sparkle without drawing too much attention. When, at the end of a climactic scene, the book soars and reaches a summit, how to continue the narration, how to come back down, without losing the reader's attention? Does the line of a book have to be a rising crescendo from start to finish? No, you can install accelerandos inside individual parts, you can play with breaks in rhythm, you can make the last line of a paragraph resound. All these things can be calculated, meted, and measured. They're technical questions, the business of craft. A book must seem self-evident to a reader, and not something premeditated or constructed. But this self-evidence is something the writer himself must construct.

Two seemingly irreconcilable notions have always been in play in writing, I think: urgency and patience.

Urgency, which calls on impulse, ardour, speed — and patience, which requires slowness, steadfastness, and effort. And yet both are indispensable to writing a book, in varying proportions, distinct doses, every writer working out an individual alchemy, one or the other of these traits being dominant and the other recessive, like alleles that decide the colour of one's eyes. And so, among writers, there are the urgent and the patient, those in whom urgency dominates (Rimbaud, Faulkner, Dostoyevsky), and those in whom patience prevails — Flaubert, of course, the very model of patience.

Usually, urgency presides over the writing of a book, and patience is but its indispensable complement, which allows for the later correction of the manuscript's early drafts. In Proust, it would seem that patience precedes urgency. Proust does not write the first draft of IN SEARCH OF LOST TIME; he simply lives, taking all the time he wants, as if reading it over before even writing it. Patience is his life and urgency his body of work. But every personal way of understanding the act of writing is a unique neurosis. Every night, Kafka would sit down at his desk and wait for the impetus that would bring him to write. He had this faith in literature, it was all he believed in, all he wanted ('I cannot nor do I want to be any other thing'), and every night he thought this inaccessible ideal — writing — would happen for him. Indeed, sometimes it did. He

E

wrote 'The Judgement' in one night, and *THE METAMORPHOSIS* would be written in the same state of grace. Beside these nights of fever and urgency, the practice of writing was, for Kafka, an arid daily quest. Nothing ever came, not ever. Day after day, he wrote in his *DIARIES*: 'Today I wrote nothing.' I loved Kafka's *DIARIES* so much; I devoured them passionately, lived on them, went back to them again and again, studied, annotated, meditated on them. Some sentences in the *DIARIES* are terrible, cruel, lucid; all are moving: 'Uncertainty, drought, silence, it will all pass away.'

## PATIENCE

In writing a book, everything always begins and ends with patience. Beforehand, the book must be left to steep in itself; in this ripening phase, the first images come to you, the characters are sketched. You gather research, take notes, work out an early plan of the whole in your head. With this preparatory phase pushed to the extreme, the danger lies in never starting the novel (Barthes' syndrome, in a way), like the narrator of *TELEVISION* who, due to exaggerated scruples and anxiety from the exigencies of perfectionism, settles for a constant state of readiness to write 'without taking the easy way out and actually doing so' (67). For, however essential it is to hold on to a text at length, letting go one day is also indispensable, after all. Afterwards, as soon as a page is finished, you print it out and read it over, amend, delete, draw arrows going every which way, correct, add a few handwritten lines, check a word, rework a few turns of phrase. Then you print the page out again and start all over, re-correct, check again, then reprint and reread, and so on, to infinity, hunting down errors and flushing out dross, until the final paring in the proofs.

I like that moment at dawn when you cautiously open the manuscript of a book in progress, in a house still asleep. There are several strategies for trying to see the work with a fresh eye, to surprise it, catch it unawares, as if seeing it for the first time, to judge it with an unbiased eye. A nap can do the trick; a good night's sleep is even better. I even suspect that part of reading a book over can happen during sleep. When you're awake, a book etches itself into the brain with the precision of a chess position, but when you sleep at night, the study of variants continues, as with a computer you leave on to examine the immensity of the calculations in play in an operation (such that sometimes the answer comes to me on waking without any particular conscious effort). But no point doggedly deleting without end; only time truly cleanses and renews one's vision. According to Palma the Younger, Titian always turned his paintings to the wall for months at a time without looking at them. Then, when he took them up again, 'he would examine them with strict attention, as if they had been his mortal enemies.' Oh, dear mortal enemies!

'How, in such conditions, can I write, to consider only the manual aspect of that bitter folly?' asks Beckett. I can't remember much now about my first typewriters: there was a little clockwork orange one on which I wrote *ÉCHECS* [Failures/Chess], my first book. But my first real typewriter, my beauty, my one and only, the thought of which still brings tears to my eyes (ah, but crocodile, of course), was my big fat Olivetti ET121 – so beautiful, so efficient, and so very sophisticated that the instructions assumed it was meant only for secretaries or professional typists and were exclusively addressed to female users ('l'utilisatrice doit faire ceci, l'utilisatrice doit faire cela') – and I complied, intimidated, delighted, blushing, trembling, giving the best of myself, with two fingers for the next ten years. With this darling machine – but what am I saying? – on this darling machine, I wrote *THE BATHROOM*, *MONSIEUR*, *CAMERA*, *RETICENCE*. Where is she now? Abandoned, I imagine – on the scrapheap. O cruel fate! I see her still, in her native splendour, that dear fat old Olivetti, sitting on my desk in Médéa when, in the early hours of that sunny afternoon in 1983, I removed it from its packaging and peeled back the kapok padding, the many layers of transparent plastic, and delicately freed it from its silk paraments and dustcover of embroidered lace (I exaggerate, but only slightly). I can see her now, sitting on the desk of my office in Médéa ready to give herself to me, black and massive, elegant, silent and unmoving, with – to prop the paper up – a transparent windshield streamlined like a 1950s Italian convertible.

These days, I only use the computer. Before setting out, I gather my things into a soft-sided overnight bag, black for a while and now a dark velvety blue, like a mobile office, a portable arsenal, which I take with me to Ostend or Corsica, with my MacBook Pro, which succeeds two white iBooks and two greyish, disappointing PowerBooks (one completely autistic, which refused to print anymore, and the other which expired in my arms with just enough time, in a dying breath, to deliver up the contents of its hard drive). I set the computer down flat in my bag, with the various wires and power cords pertaining thereto, and then I add a mouse, sometimes a keyboard, a folder with my research, a dictionary recently gone digital, and the manuscript in progress. The complete manuscripts of my last few books aren't more than fifty pages. I work on dense pages overcrowded with characters, in a Helvetica-based font with minimal line spacing, which gives very dense blocks of text, barely readable, discouraging to reread. I like it this way, because it forces me never to be content, to be ever more demanding. I must cut, clarify, simplify over and over again, those depressing blocks of text before my eyes, to make them fluid, make them fly. But I know that when the text has donned its handsomest finery, it will be put in Times New Roman, laid out meticulously on the page in nicely spaced out lines. I'll send it to Irène Lindon adorned with a cover dark blue as the night, and that poor shrivelled thing I've sweated over for months will blossom in the light like a flower opening to the sun. The idea is to train under ever harder conditions, not to know comfort till the day has come; to practice penalty kicks with ski boots on (the day you take the ski boots off, it'll be easier right away – you'll see).

I almost never take preparatory notes before beginning a book. A novel must already be underway so my thoughts can cling to an episode of an existing book, a gestating scene starting to emerge slowly from my mind, like those whitish shapes with blurry, shifting silhouettes you see showing up on ultrasounds. Notes are more for the writing phase. Sometimes, in Ostend, I stop on the dyke and exhume a notebook from my pocket, extricating it from crumpled tissues flecked with grains of sand, to scribble a few words quickly while standing on the dike in the wind and drizzle, sometimes even in a shower; how beautiful it is to see the idea I've just jotted down be instantly diluted in the rain.

> I owned a whole collection of notebooks, notepads, and scratchpads made by Rhodia or Schleicher & Schuell, with orange covers and detachable pages, as well as several little square Chinese notebooks with elegant hard covers in black and red. I always took a few of these with me when I went out, slipping them into my pocket before leaving my study, gradually filling them with bits or fragments of sentences, thoughts and aphorisms, observations and remarks (the latter being generally only the more accurate expression of the next-to-latter), which as a rule I never made use of in my actual work. No matter how brilliant, an idea really wasn't worth keeping if you couldn't even remember it without writing it down, it seemed to me. (139–40)

I wrote these words more than fifteen years ago (in Ostend, already, not far from where I'm sitting now), and I have nothing to add, except perhaps a few new notebooks to mention, my little Muji notebooks, so well-proportioned – darling little notebooks, A6 or passport-sized, supple, with charcoal or kraft paper covers – and perhaps a word on my pens, felt-tips in fact, Mitsubishi Uni-ball EYEs with tungsten carbide roller balls, fine or micro point, usually black but occasionally blue. I have an entire set fanned out on my desk (I thought I loved literature, but it was office supplies I loved, my word!).

When I was writing my first books, I worked almost without research. I wrote THE BATHROOM empty-handed: I was lent a copy of Pascal's PENSÉES, from which I wanted to translate a passage on diversion into English – and I had to borrow a high school biology textbook from a colleague for basic squid anatomy. But now, with the widespread expansion of the internet, I can access a truly encyclopaedic wealth of knowledge on any subject in real time. In THE TRUTH ABOUT MARIE, I very carefully described the piece of furniture the characters were moving out of Marie's apartment in the middle of the night: the commode. But then I realised that it wasn't really important to me to make readers see this piece of furniture in their minds. It was the

E

word itself, 'le bahut', that interested me, its scruffiness, its pleasing sound: as a literary detail, deliberate, visible, aware, and not the image it evoked, an iconic detail, to take up the distinction Daniel Arasse has proposed. In other words, it was important that readers hear the word, not that they see it. My description of the commode, which allowed readers to picture it – but added nothing to the hearing it – was thus pointless, and I deleted it.

For *THE TRUTH ABOUT MARIE*, I had to do even more research than usual, for I was tackling several themes largely unknown to me (heart attacks, horses, transporting living animals in cargo planes). For the horses, I bought an exhaustive *HORSE OWNER'S VETERINARY HANDBOOK*. But I even did that one better: I went so far as to climb on a horse and go riding in the Corsican maquis in the summer of 2006. It was the first time in my life I'd ever been on a horse (how far we sometimes go for research!). For the heart attack, I avoided having one myself (self-sacrifice has its limits), preferring to call up a doctor friend instead, and invite him to a Brussels brasserie for lunch. A bit embarrassed at the table, not daring to reveal the scene I was imagining (in general, I don't much like talking about the books I'm in the middle of writing), I asked him in a low voice, not directly but in a roundabout way, coughing slightly and rubbing my fingers, as if I had to inform him of some peculiar desiderata: whom to contact in case of a slight hiccup, for example, if a heart attack should occur right during sex? In such cases, who shows up at the apartment (police? paramedics? firemen?)? It was during this lunch that I heard for the first time that ever so risqué word, defibrillation. The experience repeated itself a few months later, when I was with an Air France captain in a restaurant – Paris, this time – and, all luncheon long, I listened attentively while filling my little notebook with adorable doodles.

## URGENCY

Urgency is fleeting, fragile, intermittent.

Urgency, as I understand it, is not inspiration. What distinguishes the two is that inspiration is received and urgency acquired. In the myth of inspiration – that great romantic myth – is a passivity I find displeasing, wherein the writer – the inspired poet – is the plaything of some grace outside himself, God or Nature, who comes and lays a finger on his innocent brow. No. Urgency is no gift, but a quest. It is acquired only through effort, built only through work; you must go to meet it, venture into its realm. For urgency indeed has a realm, an abstract, metaphorical place in those inner regions reached only after a lengthy voyage. Urgency must be attained through immersion. You dive very deep, fill your lungs with air and take a plunge, leave the everyday world behind and dive into the book underway, as if to the very ocean floor. You don't hit the bottom right away; there are steps, stages of decompression. In the early

E

phases of the descent, you can still feel the visible world above, still see it even, still draw inspiration from it. That means you're not deep enough. You have to keep going, persevere. At 130 metres, you can barely see anything anymore, and you start to make out new shadows; memories of real people fade away while fictive creatures appear and surround us, a swarm of living micro-organisms of various shapes and sizes. We are in an unsettled world between reality and fiction. We keep going down and, past 200 metres, not a single ray of sunlight reaches us. We have come at last to the realm of urgency, the world of abysses, more than 300 million square kilometres of darkness and silence where crushing pressure reigns and endless blind presences proliferate, infinitesimal potential lives in motion. Here we are: this is the right depth, we have the necessary distance, the ideal detachment to reconstruct the world – to reproduce, in the very depths of writing, everything we have taken in on the surface. Here, at the very heart of urgency, everything comes easily, floats free and lets go, actual sight is of no more use to us, but the inner eye widens, and a fictive, fabulous world appears in our minds. Our senses are alert, our perceptions heightened, sensitivity intensified; there's a tipping over, and everything comes gushing out, sentences are born, flow, fall over each other, and everything is right, everything works out, everything gathers and fits together in this intimate darkness that is the inside of our very minds. But the tiniest thing – a speck of dust, the unforeseen – derails the whole process and brings us back up to the surface: for urgency is fragile, and can escape us at any moment.

Urgency is a state of writing that can only be arrived at after infinite patience. It is the reward for that patience, the miraculous denouement. All the efforts we made in the name of our book were, in reality, only straining toward this singular moment when urgency bursts forth, when it all tips over, when it comes by itself, when the thread never stops unwinding from the ball. As in tennis after hours of practice in which every movement has been analysed, broken down, and put back together ad infinitum, but remains stiff, rigid, and soulless, there comes a moment, in the heat of a match, when you start letting your strokes go and pull off some things that would've been unimaginable before you'd warmed up, and were only made possible by the rigour and tenacity of the training session that came beforehand. At moments like these, in the heat of writing, there's nothing we can't try, everything works; we graze the net, we brush the lines, we find everything instinctively, every bodily posture, the ideal bend to the knee, the way to wind up and swing – everything is right, every image, every word, every adjective caught in mid-air and put back into play – everything finds its exact place in the book.

That's all there is to writing a book: this alternation between phases of gush and perseverance. After weeks of being blocked while I was writing THE TRUTH ABOUT MARIE, suddenly Zahir was fleeing down the runway at Narita. The scansion that set in then; the words that raced out, driving forward, dashing after the purebred;

the jerky, staccato rhythm of the sentence calqued on the horse's gallop — these have something to do with breathlessness. We — the author, the reader, the pursuers, the sentence – are literally breathless. Beside these scenes written in urgency are moments when all forward progress stops, when the winds have fallen, and we are irreparably becalmed. That is when you must persevere, hang on, grit your teeth, keep not getting there, for urgency keeps moving forward, keeps working unconsciously, building up energy. There's always something exponential about writing a book; the third month of work is enriched by the preceding ones. The more constant the effort has been, the more intense the relief will be. You might even further whet the necessity of urgency by restraining your desire, constraining it, pulling it back like a rubber band in a deliberate strategy of retention, in order to lend its forward momentum all possible power, so that when the dykes burst, the book sweeps everything upon its flood.

E

# POEMS

BY

# NAJWAN DARWISH

(*tr.* SOUSAN HAMMAD
AND ANDREW NANCE)

## A REFUGEE FROM CRETE

I am a refugee from Crete
I practice the art of tea-drinking:
infusing with mint on summer days
and sage on winter nights
Each time a language shelters me
I escape into its sister's bosom
until I am a seducer of languages

I am a refugee from Crete
I have only songs I have forgotten
and some souvenirs:
a handful of salt is my mother's voice
a bird's feather is my father's tear
and the swings of the children who were
slaughtered by no one
I offer this to you
in exchange for pennies or a loaf of bread

I am a refugee from Crete.

# زير لغات

أنا لاجئٌ من كُريتْ
أحترفُ شُرب الشاي
بالنعنع في أيام الصَّيف
وبالميرَميَّة في ليالي الشتاء.
كلَّما آوتني لغةٌ
فَرَرتُ إلى حضْنِ أختها
حتَّى صِرتُ زيرَ لُغات.


أنا لاجئٌ من كريت
لا أَملِكُ سوى أُغنيات نسيتُها
وبِضعَ تذكارات:
حَفْنةُ مِلحٍ هي صوتُ أمي
ريشةُ عصفور أظُنُّها دمعة أبي
وأراجيحُ أطفالٍ ذُبحوا "من تلقاء أنفسهم"
أعرضها عليكم
لقاء بِضْعةِ قُروشٍ أو رغيف!


.     .     .     .


أنا لاجئٌ من كريت.

## CARGO OF SEVEN CAMELS

The singer is exhausted from longing
in each of her moans
          is a cargo of seven camels
in each chorus
          a tribe migrates
and her silence is a city
where everyone is asleep and she is awake
but what about my moans that have no weight
and my chorus that has no fame
and my silence is a city
where the invaders prevent our arrival.

## حِمْل سبعة جِمال

المغنّية مُنْهَكة مِنْ الشوق
في كلِّ آهةٍ حِمْل سبعة جِمال
في كلّ ترجيعةٍ هجرةُ قبيلة
وصمتُها مدينةٌ نام جميع سكانها وهي مستيقظة.
لكن ماذا أصنع أنا الذي لا وزن لآهتي
ولا صيت لترجيعاتي
وصمتي مدينةٌ
مَنَعَ الغزاةُ وصولنا إليها.

## FOR MA'TOUB LOUNÈS

The route from Haifa to Jerusalem is your final album
and I drive in darkness
transported by your voice, o Ma'toub Lounès

The Mediterranean is on my right
and I don't know which vocal cord
drives my vehicle
I don't think about your bleeding paradise
o Algeria
you're more than a mirage


My breath suffocates also
against those
and them
Do you really think they can tell the difference
between the hills of Tizi Ouzou
and the plains of Hauran?

The route from Haifa to Jerusalem is your final album
and I drive in darkness.

إلى معطوب لوَنَّاس


الطريق مِنْ حيفا إلى القُدس اسطوانتك الأخيرة
وأنا أسوق في الظلام
محمولاً على صوتك يا معطوب لوَنَّاس..


المتوسِّطُ عن يميني ولا أعرف أية عُرَبٍ صوتيةٍ تَدفع مركبتي
ولا أعود أُفكِّر
إلا بفردوسكِ الدامي أيتها الجزائر السَّراب


أنفاسي المخنوقة أيضاً، ضد هؤلاء وهؤلاء.
أتظنهم حقاً يميِّزون بين هضبات "تيزي وزُّو" وسهول "حوران"؟


الطريق من القدس إلى حيفا اسطوانتك الأخيرة
وأنا أسوق في الظلام  .

## I AM JUST A FERRYBOAT

I am just a ferryboat in Haifa
amused with the sun and rhythms
awaiting you

Every day I whistle
but never depart

I am just a storm
turning loose debris
thinking of a brood of birds
on a tree

I am you
you return but don't ask about me?
*How could you?*
I release a distant 'why'
Set aside for you
in the hailstorm that strikes the shore

in this ship that docks at the edge
of your arrival

**مجرّد باخرة**


أنا مجرَّد باخرة في حيفا
تلعب مع الشمس والزرقة وتنتظركم .


كل يوم تصفر ولا تغادر .


أنا مجرّد عاصفة تفكِّر بفراخ العصافير في الشجر وتتقطّع
أنا أنتم
ترجعون ولا تسألون عنّي؟ "ولو" كبيرةٌ أُخبِئها منذ الآن، في البَرَد يضرب الشاطيء
في هذه الباخرة المنتهية عند حافة وصولكم.

## BINT JBEIL

My images and allegories are sleeping in beds,
broken and sick and I can do nothing, broken
before dawn in front of the TV, trying to pray
for those who are defending Bint Jbeil tonight.
How could he pray, he who believes in nothing?
After a while, dawn will expose the murders,
and I will go to sleep broken down by the amount
of debt I carry for those who raised dawn another day
on the hills of Bint Jbeil.

بنت جبيل

كانت استعاراتي وصوري وكناياتي نائماتٍ في الأسرّة، مكسوراتٍ ومريضات.
وأنا لا أَلوي على شيء
قُبيْل الفَجْرِ مكسوراً أمام التلفزيون، أُحاول أن أُصلّي للذين يدافعون الليلةَ عن بِنْت جبيل.

[كيف يصلّي الذي لا يؤمن بشيء؟]

بعد قليلٍ يُسْفِرُ الفَجرُ عن القتلى
وأذهبَ أنا للنوم مكسوراً أمام حَجْمِ الدَّين الذي أحمله
للذين رفعوا الفجرَ يوماً آخرَ على "تلّات" بنت جبيل.

## DREAMS OF OTHERS

Asian chefs are cooking the sun and sousing it with wine,
and you are quarreling in the dreams that continue
even after you wake up in the afternoon.
I thought you were strong enough; I thought you did not need
to stab someone, to punch someone, to escape from someone...

These are the dreams of others, which you carry instead.
Dreams of weaklings clinging to their pillows while
sleeping in bleak hotels, dreams of waiters
and desperate bartenders...

These are the dreams of others,
yours were stolen.

## أحلام آخرين

طهاةٌ آسيويّون يطبخون الشّمس ويرنِّخونها بالنبيذ
وأنت تتشاجر في الأحلام التي تستمرّ حتى بعد استيقاظك في الظهيرة
كنتُ أحسبك قويّاً لدرجةٍ لا حاجة معها لِلُكْم أحدٍ أو طعن أحدٍ أو الهرب مِنْ أحد...
هذي أحلام آخرين تحملها عنهم
أحلام ضعفاء تشبَّثوا بوسائدهم وهم ينامون في فنادق كئيبة
أحلام نُدُلٍ
وساقيات مشارب يائسات
...

هذي أحلام آخرين... وأحلامك سُرِقت.

# WHAT CAN AN ART MAGAZINE BE?

BY

## ORIT GAT

WHAT CAN AN ART MAGAZINE BE? Today, as the publishing industry re-assesses its role in the age of the internet, the pioneering art magazine METRONOME provides an example of how a print publication can engage with a community of readers and contributors. While online publishing allows for ambitious publications that cater to a small audience, the ability of the web to reach anyone, anywhere makes such small-scale operations seem futile or unambitious. The internet has modified our understanding of what publics are and can be: when distribution brings with it larger discussions about discourse and its limitations not because of physical accessibility, but because of a lack of shared points of access, the real achievement – and legacy – of a small magazine is in its provision of a space for dialogue rather than its creation of a public. This is a useful example – if not the ultimate one – for considering publishing as a curatorial practice. And with that, to suggest that the production of art magazines, both in print and online, can be a more nuanced, more open practice than the role assigned to it in the incessant conversations about the current state of publishing.

The director of one of the very few libraries in the United States to keep copies of METRONOME emails me: 'There are twelve issues total for METRONOME,' she writes. 'The first issue in 1996 begins with "0" rather than "1" – one of the eccentricities of the publication.' She attaches the library records, which include the following notes: 'Edited Clémentine Deliss. Publication inter-culturelle des arts plastiques = Inter-cultural publication of the visual arts. Four no. a year. Later issues vary in size, format, and languages.'

Issue 0 of METRONOME was published in 2,000 copies in 1996, in Dakar. Its first editorial read: 'METRONOME is the first edition of a new series of intercultural publications produced from Dakar and London. It proposes a debate from within the visual arts, interpolating artists, critics, philosophers, historians, aestheticians, curators, patrons, and art enthusiasts.' At the time, Deliss, now director of the Weltkulturen Museum in Frankfurt, had just curated an exhibition at Whitechapel Gallery as part of Africa '95, a season focused on contemporary art from Africa, of which she was the artistic director. She then stopped organising shows and came to define herself, as she puts it in a letter to Judith Ickowitz which serves as the editorial to METRONOME 9, as a 'curator who realised that exhibitions were not her medium'. Deliss's objective to disseminate new ideas by artists working in diverse locations led her to a particular and to my knowledge unprecedented way of working: each issue of METRONOME was produced in a different place, following a period of research on site with artists and writers she met there. Production – including printing – also took place locally. Twelve issues of METRONOME were printed between 1996 and 2007 in locations including Dakar, Berlin, Basel, Vienna, Frankfurt, Oslo, Copenhagen, Portland, and Tokyo. Metronome Press, which Deliss founded with curator Thomas Boutoux in 2005, has published four novels, including the first edition of Tom McCarthy's REMAINDER.

E

*METRONOME* wasn't a reflection of the places in which it was produced nor did it seek to provide an analysis of the visual works it included. What it aspired to offer was a critical locus for discourse. *METRONOME* o was still marked with some attributes recognisable from other periodicals – it was introduced as the pilot issue for a new quarterly and had a price on its cover. While the first three issues (Dakar, 1996; London, 1997; Berlin, 1997) had a similar look – all large format with stapled pages, where visuals alone took over the front and text followed – later editions diverged from that structure. *METRONOME 3* (Basel, 1997) was a documentation of an event, Tempolabor, a conference about the labour of creative workers that took place at Kunsthalle Basel. Designed like an old-fashioned book whose pages had to be cut by hand, it included original work by artists and writers, as well as the edited transcript of Deliss's attempt to draw together some unfinished conversations between artists and writers by inviting thirty-nine people to Basel for four days of discussion (among the participants were artists and curators including Charles Esche, Olaf Nicolai and Nicolaus Schafhausen). *METRONOME 4-5-6* (Edinburgh, Bordeaux, Frankfurt, Vienna, Biella, 1999) were compiled into one book-form issue, entitled 'Backwards Translation', that attempted to serve as a reference encyclopaedia for artists and artistic producers today; and *METRONOME 7* (Scandinavia, 2001) was a book and a CD, designed by Liam Gillick, which included interviews between Deliss and artists including Karl Holmqvist, Bjarne Melgaard and Ingrid Luche.

*METRONOME* was a very particular publication: it never had a fixed identity, format, or even an address; a large section of each issue was dedicated to visuals; and the texts did not necessarily discuss visual art, but engaged the field of cultural production surrounding contemporary art – theory, philosophy, and criticism, but also fiction and experimental writing. In the spectrum of art publications *METRONOME* falls far from the *ARTFORUM*s of the world, and as such expands the possibilities of a hybrid curatorial and editorial practice. An art magazine can be a platform for discussions in a way that exhibitions can't be: because it allows writers and artists a space for reflection rather than presentation, but also because its serialised nature enables conversations that develop over time and for a reassessment or reaction to previous issues, and lastly, since a printed magazine does not have a fixed duration, unlike an exhibition.

*METRONOME*'s free form allowed artists, writers, and critics a space for in-depth consideration of subjects as diverse as art education, the role of fiction and literature in art, and translation and globalisation, while also encouraging a cross-cultural exchange by its particular attitude to the geography of publishing. Deliss's emphasis on the local nature of the magazine also made it into a very intimate stage for sharing ideas, one enhanced by another distinct characteristic of the magazine: it was never formally distributed. Every contributor to the magazine received a large number of copies to circulate as they saw fit. All of which contrast it most sharply with one thing – the internet.

¶In the last few years, a good deal of critical research has been directed at the history of publishing in the arts (books by Gwen Allen and Philip E. Aaron & Andrew Roth among them), but it has focused on artists' publications while the print initiatives of curators have gone mostly unnoticed. This is surprising at a moment when new magazines are added to the curatorial bookshelf (for example, THE EXHIBITIONIST and MANIFESTA JOURNAL, both of which attempt to theorise and historicise the practice of curating). But there is little room in these publications for content or editorial lines that address the proximity of the editorial space to the curatorial one, which would seem useful at a time when the definition of curating is constantly being expanded – not by the overuse of the word 'curated', as in 'curated wine list', but rather, through the inflation of participants in curatorial endeavours.

Deliss's idea of curating without working on exhibitions suggests a useful, less wine-list-y definition of what curating could be. She has definitely sketched that in METRONOME, where the separation between text and visuals (so that images are independent and do not act as illustrations) and the collaborative working process are systematic for her thinking of the magazine as a curatorial project. When comparing METRONOME to other curator-initiated publications, the fact that it has a different aspiration stands out: not to discuss an artistic scene, but be part of it; not to provide a reflection on art and curating, but to advance another space for these to be produced.

In that, METRONOME seems closer in spirit to artists's magazines like ASPEN and AVALANCHE. The first, published in the 1960s in New York City, is an oft-cited example that has won a cult following: each issue of ASPEN consisted of a boxed set of ephemera including objects such as vinyl records, super-8 reels, and postcards. It featured writers and artists like Brian O'Doherty, John Cage and Yoko Ono, and is now so revered that it is pretty regularly displayed in vitrines in the context of exhibitions like the MATERIALIZING SIX YEARS: LUCY LIPPARD AND THE EMERGENCE OF CONCEPTUAL ART show at the Brooklyn Museum in 2012. AVALANCHE, published between 1970–76 by Liza Bear and Willoughby Sharp, was meant to be a gallery in a magazine and focused on presenting new work and contextualising it only with interviews and descriptions of artists' processes. In thirteen issues of AVALANCHE its pages included the work of Vito Acconci (to whom issue six was dedicated), Bruce Nauman, Yvonne Rainer and Joseph Beuys (who was on the cover of issue one).

Both ASPEN and AVALANCHE are identified with a certain New York scene – and contributed to its myth creation, especially in the case of AVALANCHE, the covers of which featured portraits of artists, always in black and white, always close-up, in a way comparable to musicians and movie stars. But, as is the case for METRONOME,

E

they did not intend merely to reflect an art scene but to partake in it: both magazines launched artistic and editorial careers and created, as well as documented, moments, movements and tendencies in art that continue to be of interest to curators and art historians today. They also contributed to the production and dissemination of knowledge beyond geographical borders (one manifest example: Barthes' 'Death of the Author' was first published in *ASPEN* in 1967).

The ongoing bid to historicise contemporary art has led to the aforementioned wave of new research on art publications, both as primary information for research on artists, but also as a way to broaden our understanding of the context in which artworks are made. A similar move is currently being made to analyse the records of curatorial practice. (This could be the academic contribution that the inflating number of curatorial studies programmes provide us with.) As part of said research, and in a comparable way to the study of art magazines as a way to further our understanding of artistic practice, we should be looking at publishing as a curatorial medium. This, in turn, would lead us to question what an audience or public is, and what it could be.

What does it mean for a curator to eschew the aspiration to enlarge his or her audience? For *METRONOME*, this is a point of strength – knowing your audience personally brings you closer to engaging with it in a very immediate way. Distributing the magazine informally, on the basis of personal relationships, was a decision that came to define the nature of *METRONOME*. And in a somewhat incongruous way, even its limited distribution was democratic in that the magazine was collaborative in its nature and relied on a sort of gift economy for its dissemination. In addition to that, every number included a list of the previous issues and their content: if you encounter one issue (granted, usually in a very particular visual arts context) you know who, when and where each preceding issue of *METRONOME* was produced. One result of the strong authorship of Deliss's editorial process is the awareness of the identity of the readership, which allows the creation of an intimate, long-standing dialogue. While it may be tempting to tie together the idea of opening up to a larger public with a certain democratic largesse, the public of more inclusive and less open-ended visual arts initiatives would have much less of an agency than the limited public exposed to *METRONOME*. This may indicate *METRONOME*'s successful specificity: that the production of a single issue of the magazine is also a complex method for building knowledge collaboratively.

So *METRONOME* encourages dialogue, but only between a limited number of people in a particular field. Today it remains largely unavailable, which seems para-doxical when considering that, ideally, the publication's audience should have been as dispersed as its identity was. The question of accessibility and elitism is important when considering *METRONOME*: Could a magazine really inform artistic discourse when it comes out sporadically and retains a separatist attitude? Is it possible to inspire

E

dialogue without allowing people into the conversation?

These are complex questions for any curator, but they are further complicated in the context of a magazine, especially when surveying the possibilities offered by the internet for contemporary art publishing. Offering content online, free and open to all, seems like the antithesis of what METRONOME did. But its particular attitude towards print and distribution could still be a model as curators, editors and readers reassess what we do with publishing online. The relationship between the print and online presence of magazines is an ongoing discussion at editorial meetings and has led to numerous strategies – from identical print and online versions, through separate mobile apps, and up to the creation of unique content for print and web. For publishing, the internet seems both the most natural environment and a dizzying array of possibilities. Then why print magazines? And why do we see many online magazines print out the internet, launching either a print-on-demand system (E-FLUX JOURNAL) or a series of readers (both E-FLUX JOURNAL and TRIPLE CANOPY are good examples) reproducing their online content in printed form?

Part of this has to do with attention. While publishing online allows for any given piece to be multitextual by hyperlinking, the links send a reader away from any given text. The solitude that a print publication allows with its content is irreplaceable online. (This solitude is not unequivocally a good thing: it may satisfy advertisers, and allow for more coherent delivery of information in print, but it also limits the reader's scope of references and ignores the kind of curiosity we have come to develop online, constantly checking for facts, accumulating further reading material, generating individualised networks of interests that stem from a given piece.) Print provides a more stable archive that would not be subjected to expired URLs and allow for conservation in libraries. It's also, though, the weight of history. A magazine looks to its predecessors, wants to belong to a certain tradition. And that tradition, at least at the moment, is in print. And the possibilities of print as a medium are one of the central things a publication like METRONOME explores. Only print allows for projects like METRONOME. The more we look at screens, the more information we consume online, the more we value immediacy and connectivity – whereas a publication like METRONOME lingers on the local, the process, the ongoing. And its informal distribution is based on a physical object that can be handed out, discussed, and preserved.

One of the outcomes of the ongoing discourse of online versus offline publishing is that it brought about a very close consideration of why we publish. In the visual arts, there's this great tradition (or cliché) of artists, critics, and curators discussing their first encounter with the art of their generation on the pages of a magazine. (For a recent example, see Bob Nickas's column in ARTFORUM's November 2013 issue, in which he wrote about being in middle school and discovering Robert Smithson via the cover of the September 1969 issue of ARTFORUM.) We don't need that anymore. No one sneaks copies of contemporary art magazines past the Iron Curtain. No teenager in the periphery of the art world needs glossy pages and high–resolution images. For that, we have the internet. But for models, we have print. We should be looking at historical precedents, and the example of *METRONOME* – with its focus on locality at a time of rapid globalisation, on proximity and familiarity at an age of online reader-ship, and its commitment to working on a small scale – provides one strategy through which to think of the future of publishing in the face of some instincts that the internet provokes in us: to work on too large a scale, and too quickly.

E

# MIRIAM

BY

# GREG BAXTER

I GOT THE NEWS about Miriam's death first, before my father. The Berlin police telephoned me. I was walking into a meeting with the firm – an aerospace firm – that has taken me on to run a project for them. Though I was still officially a consultant, I'd be working on site five days a week, and the contract was for two years. The meeting was a kind of induction. Some people from the Paris office were over – the firm was headquartered in Paris – so there'd be lunch afterwards. This was just over three weeks ago. It was a cold morning in London. Just as I was about to walk into the meeting, my phone rang. I was going to ignore it, but the number was not a UK number, it was a German number, and I thought it might possibly be Miriam – and since she never telephoned, it had to be an emergency. I excused myself and took the call. It obviously wasn't Miriam, and at first I couldn't make out who it was or what it was about. I walked toward a window – I had a view of a little laneway. On the line was a very sympathetic-sounding policewoman. She asked if it was me. I said it was. I had never gotten a phone call from the police in my life. The woman explained that Miriam had died. I do not remember how I responded. I do remember asking, at some point, Has my father been told? She didn't say anything right away, and I realised that if he had been told first, it would have been him on the phone, not the Berlin police, so I changed my question to a statement, which was just me thinking out loud. I said, I guess I will have to inform my dad now. Again, she waited, she said nothing. The meeting room was filling up. I could sense, without even seeing it – I had walked a long way to find the window I was looking out – that everybody was seated around the table already, trying to look prepared or eager by flipping through papers. I could hear some chatter, low, subdued, but it was coming from everywhere. The way an office sounds. It was the beginning of the week. Finally I asked the policewoman, How did you locate me? She answered, and she spoke of death notification procedures in general, and I listened very carefully. I decided I would like to know these things in order to explain them to my father. I thought my father might become emotional and I wouldn't have the slightest idea how to deal with it, except to offer, as a pill for any pain he might feel, a diversion into the eccentricities of death notifications in Germany. I have such a vivid memory of staring at that little laneway while the policewoman spoke. She was patient and polite, and at some point during her explanation I realised that I would have to travel to Berlin, and so would my father. I would be seeing my father for the first time in six years, and this time Miriam would be there, in a manner of speaking.

During the policewoman's explanation, a man crept up behind me, stopped a bit short, and whispered, loud enough to make it impossible to ignore him, Everything okay? I turned around and straightened up, and I was going to give him a thumbs-up and a smile, but then I saw he was pointing at his wrist, at the watch on his wrist, and he was irritated. Everything okay? he said again, but louder. I did not smile, but I held up two fingers and silently said, Two minutes. When the policewoman finished her explanation of death notifications, she turned her attention to our case, to Miriam. She had been discovered in her apartment. They had gone through her personal effects and found my contact details. A coroner's inquest would follow as a matter of procedure, and then the body, Miriam's body, would be released. How long? I asked. Not long, she said. Even though it did turn out to be long, I don't think the policewoman was lying. It was just that *not long* meant something different to her than it meant to me. I asked what would happen once the body was released, and she gave me the contact details of somebody in the American embassy who had already been fully briefed, and who had asked that I call as soon as possible. That turned out to be Trish. I hung up. I went into the meeting room and told everybody I was sorry for the delay. There were no questions about the call, but there was a woman in the room who looked like she was going to ask, politely, if I needed to go home. In the room sat the director of sales and marketing, the senior marketing manager, two senior sales managers – one of whom was the man who came out to the corridor to hasten me – and this woman, the one who seemed a little bit different from the rest, possibly from human resources, I can't remember. The meeting room was in a refurbished part of a grand old building, and the walls of the room were glass, and we could see, and be seen by, several people working in other glass enclosures around us. I had been briefed about the project I'd been hired to work on, but now they gave me a more specific briefing. I offered some ideas I'd been developing. The director of marketing was a woman with a French name but a London accent. She had short grey hair. She was reassuringly intelligent. The senior marketing manager was younger than me, probably in her late twenties. The two sales managers – both men, one was short with red hair and one was tall with black hair – wore identical suits, and were either terrified of the director of marketing or hated her, but it was easy to see that without her leadership they'd have been lost. With every sentence I spoke, the woman who might have been in human resources seemed more and more disappointed in me. As a result, I became more and more disappointed in myself. The meeting ended, and everyone seemed satisfied, and I was surprised to find myself thinking that the presentation had been more convincing for the numbed manner with which I had delivered it. So I was weirdly excited to have passed the first hurdle so successfully and also, simultaneously, experiencing acute and brief paroxysms of devastation and anxiety. The lunch was to take place at a French restaurant I didn't know. Presumably the folks from the Paris office knew it and liked it. Presumably it would be outrageously expensive. We would eat and eat and eat. The wine we would order would be unaffordable without business expensing, and even though it would be magnificent, we would all pretend it was merely adequate, and that we were accustomed to wine of that standard. I thought these things when they told me the name of the place – which I have forgotten – and

F

they all turned out to be true. We ate so much we all felt sick. We had several courses and desserts, and we got drunk, especially the London team. The men and women from the Paris team were incredibly handsome, and they made the London team seem physically repellent – they would have done so to almost any nationality. They really were some of the most beautiful people I'd ever seen. The English, said one of the French guys in the toilets – he was standing by the urinal, unzipping his trousers, and I was washing my hands, looking up at him through the mirror – are a deformed and revolting race. I smiled. I have no idea if he knew I was American, and thought it might be funny to insult the English, or if he thought I was English, and wanted to let me know, in private, how much my face disgusted him. In any case, I told him I couldn't argue, not if he were comparing the English to the French. My mother was beautiful – of Scottish descent, way back. It was too bad Miriam and I didn't look more like her.

Between my induction meeting and the lunch, I took a walk. The director of sales and marketing wanted me to tour around the place and meet some of the staff, find out what they did and why they did it, but I wanted to call my father and the embassy in Berlin. I apologised and assured her it was quite important that I make a telephone call to the US, and promised to meet everyone at the restaurant. Outside, the day was still cold, still windy, still overcast. I thought it might rain, but I don't believe – when I try to remember – that it did. Or if it did, it must have been very light rain. I walked much further than I expected to walk. I walked out the doors of the building where the aerospace firm was and pulled my phone out, but I didn't make the call. I put the phone back in my pocket and walked up towards Covent Garden, then a little bit further, winding around, looking in shop windows, looking into cafés and businesses. I hadn't consciously intended to walk to Bedford Square when I started out. I just kept making turns that led me in its direction. I just kept considering and rejecting, for no real reason, all the quiet spots I came across, all the spots from which I could have made a phone call. Bedford Square is a place I've always had a strange attraction to, and I'm sure that at some point during my walk a voice inside my head said, Well, I guess we're heading to Bedford Square again. I hadn't been there for a year or so, ever since the last time I met a woman I was seeing.

The park in Bedford Square is off limits to non-residents, but there are a few benches just outside the black wrought-iron fence that surrounds the park. The woman I had an affair with mysteriously had a key – I think it was because she worked for the British Museum. I sat for a moment on one of those benches, but it was so cold that I got up and began to pace around the park very slowly. The square was, as it always is, exceptionally quiet. The trees are immense, and even though the park was wintery and the trees had no leaves, the branches scattered way up high and dominated the view of the sky. I stared for a while, right up at them. It's still strange, to me, after all the times I've visited, to find such a pleasant and untrampled section of London less than a few blocks from Oxford Street and Tottenham Court Road, which can feel, at certain times of day, like hell on earth. You can find quiet squares all over Bloomsbury. Places nobody knows about, or places too dull to visit. Bedford Square was one of the first places where I sat down and thought, I'm in London, and for that reason it acquired a sacred status in my thoughts. As I paced, slowly, around the outside of the park, I took the phone out, went over what I might say to my father, then called. It rang about five times. My father usually picks up immediately. Suddenly I remembered the time difference. It was six in the morning there. I hung up. A moment later my phone was ringing. It was my father calling me back. I didn't answer. I suddenly could not think of a way to tell him. I'd need another couple of hours. I stopped pacing, because now I felt really foolish for not having stayed with the marketing director and toured the office with her. I stood very still and thought about hurrying back. But I had been walking for a while, and it actually wasn't long until lunch began. I could head to the restaurant, get there a few minutes early, have a drink. I watched a grey Mercedes take a very, very long time to park in a space that was probably too small for it. A man stepped out. I could not see his face, but he had silver hair. He examined his parking job, decided he did not approve, and got back in to do it again. I walked to a different corner of the park, so I would not have to watch. I called the number I'd been given for the woman in the US embassy in Berlin. Trish answered. She was professional but warm, and asked how I was coping. Well, I said, it's a shock, though I haven't seen her in years, we spoke less than I'd have liked to. Trish said, It's difficult to keep in touch when you live in different countries. I said, I never went to Berlin to see her, I should have. Trish didn't respond, and I said, Listen, sorry, in the shock of everything I forgot to ask the policewoman how Miriam died. Trish said, Are you asking me to tell you now?

I suppose, I said, if you know.

Trish told me what the police had told her, that she died of malnourishment, that she had starved. Trish said this matter-of-factly, without any weakness in her voice. Oh, I said. Trish said, Did you know she was having difficulties? No, I said, I didn't. But that was not the truth.

This is an excerpt from *MUNICH AIRPORT*, forthcoming from Penguin Ireland in July 2014.

F

# APPENDIX

JOSHUA ABELOW is an artist based in New York. Karma (New York) recently published the artist's first monograph, *ART FICTION*, which features paintings, drawings, photography and poetry.

BENEDICT ANDREWS is an Australian theatre and opera director now resident in Iceland. This year, his first collection of poetry *LENS FLARE* will be published by Pitt Street Poetry in Australia and his first volume of plays by Oberon Books in the UK. www.benedictandrews.com

NICOLA BARKER's nine previous novels include *DARKMANS* (shortlisted for the 2007 Booker and Ondaatje prizes, and winner of the Hawthornden) and *WIDE OPEN* (winner of the 2000 IMPAC Dublin Literary Award). Her tenth – *IN THE APPROACHES* – will be published in June by 4th Estate.

JACOB BROMBERG is a poet, translator, and contributing editor to *THE WHITE REVIEW*. He co-wrote the text of 'Grosse Fatigue', winner of the 2013 Venice Biennale Silver Lion, sporadically supplies 'literary clip art' via Twitter, and is currently working on two short films and a series of video poems.

NAJWAN DARWISH is a poet, critic and literary editor. He lives in Jerusalem, Palestine. He has published five books, and his selected poems in English – entitled *NOTHING MORE TO LOSE* – are published by the New York Review of Books in April 2014. In 2009, the Hay Festival Beirut39 named him one of the 39 best Arab writers under 39.

LAURA ELLIOTT work has recently appeared in *TENDER* and *3:AM*. Based in London, she is currently training to be a librarian, and co-edits *LIGHTHOUSE* literary journal.

ORIT GAT is a writer based in New York. Her writing appears regularly on *RHIZOME*, where she is a contributing editor, as well as in *FRIEZE*, *LEAP*, *ARTREVIEW*, *THE BROOKLYN RAIL* and *MODERN PAINTERS*, where she was senior editor until 2013.

EDWARD GAUVIN's translations include *A LIFE ON PAPER* by Georges-Olivier Châteaureynaud, *THE CONDUCTOR AND OTHER TALES* by Jean Ferry, and publications in *CONJUNCTIONS*, *WORLD LITERATURE TODAY*, *TIN HOUSE* and the *HARVARD REVIEW*, among others. The winner of the John Dryden Translation Prize, he is the contributing editor for Francophone comics at *WORDS WITHOUT BORDERS*. He maintains a website at edwardgauvin.com/blog.

SOUSAN HAMMAD is a writer, translator, and journalist who divides her time between France, America and Palestine. She holds a Master's degree in Cultural Translation and a Bachelor's in Journalism from the American University in Paris. www. sousanhammad.com

WILLIAM E. JONES is an artist and filmmaker who in recent years has turned to writing. His books include *Tearoom* (2008), *"Killed": Rejected Images of the Farm Security Administration* (2010), *Halsted Plays Himself* (2011), *Imitation of Christ* (2013), and *Flesh and the Cosmos* (2014). He lives in Los Angeles.

RYE DAG HOLMBOE is a writer and Ph.D. candidate in History of Art at University College, London. He  has recently co-authored and co-edited the book *JocJonJosch: Hand in Foot*, published by the Sion Art Museum, Switzerland (2013). He has recently edited *Jolene*, an artist's book which brings together the works of the poet Rachael Allen and the photographer Guy Gormley, which will be published later this year. His writings have appeared in *The White Review*, *Art Licks* and in academic journals.

CHRIS KRAUS is the author of four novels, most recently *Summer of Hate*, and two books of cultural criticism. Her monograph *Lost Properties*, on conceptual art and economic activism, was published by Semiotexte this year as part its contribution to The Whitney Biennial. She lives in LA.

ANDREW NANCE is an American poet and writer; he received an MFA from the Iowa Writers' Workshop, where he was a Truman Capote Fellow. He has taught poetry at Victoria University's International Institute of Modern Letters in Wellington, New Zealand. He is the editor of *Company* (companyjournal.org), a journal of new poetry and visual art.

MARK PRINCE is an English artist and writer living in Berlin. He writes about art for various publications.

VIDYAN RAVINTHIRAN is the Keasbey Research Fellow at Selwyn College, Cambridge. His first book of verse, *Grun-tu-molani*, is published by Bloodaxe.

WESLEY ROTHMAN's poems have appeared or are forthcoming in *32 Poems*, *Asheville Poetry Review*, *The Awl*, *Connotation Press*, *Crab Orchard Review*, *Drunken Boat*, among others. He has worked with Copper Canyon Press, *Ploughshares*, *Narrative*, and *Tupelo Quarterly*, and teaches writing and cultural literatures at Suffolk University and Emerson College.

JEAN-PHILIPPE TOUSSAINT is the author of ten novels, and the winner of numerous literary prizes, including the Prix Décembre for *THE TRUTH ABOUT MARIE*. 'Urgency and Patience' is the title essay from a forthcoming collection with Dalkey Archive Press.

ISABELLE WENZEL, born in 1982 in Wuppertal, lives and works in Amsterdam. She studied photography from 2008–2010 at the Gerrit Rietveld Akademy in Amsterdam. She has received grants from the European Photo Exhibition Award, the Körber-Stiftung Hamburg in 2011 and the Mondriaan Fonds in 2013, amongst others. Her work has been widely exhibited.

DAVID WINTERS is a literary critic and journalist. He has written for the *TLS*, the *GUARDIAN*, the *INDEPENDENT*, the *LOS ANGELES REVIEW OF BOOKS* and elsewhere.